HALLOWEEN BOO

A STEAMY HALLOWEEN NOVELLA

SARAH SPADE

1

A ROSE PETAL

Dani

So, I think my apartment is haunted.

It sounds crazy. I know it does. If anyone else told me they thought their new place was haunted, I'd laugh and then google the number of a local shrink before backing away slowly. Ghosts don't exist.

Right? *Wrong.* They're definitely real—at least, my Casper is.

It all started with a rose petal.

I work for a marketing firm that's based in Massachusetts. Having been born and raised in California, it was a shock for me to relocate to Salem at the beginning of this year. Even though the money and the promotion were totally worth it, it meant I had to leave my family and friends back in Palo Alto.

Thing is, apart from weekend business trips into Boston, I knew nothing about living in the Northeast. So my bosses partnered me with another girl in my department.

Allison Shaw.

Like me, Allison was stationed out of the Salem offices and, having grown up in the area, she was tasked with helping me find an apartment to live in since it was pointless to stay in a hotel year-round.

I don't know why exactly she recommended my place. It's in a nice part of town, on the outskirts where it's easy to avoid all the witchy tourist nonsense. Having never been a big fan of Halloween—and a firm non-believer in the supernatural—moving to Salem was a way bigger culture shock.

And let's not even talk about my first Massachusetts winter. I was lucky to survive *that*.

Anyway.

The rose petal.

I moved into the apartment in the end of January. Apart from Allison, I never had any company though, looking back on it, I think I always sensed that I wasn't exactly alone.

The apartment never seemed empty, even when it was just me, my e-reader, my television in the background, and a mug of hot chocolate to keeping me from freezing my tits off.

Did I mention that winter in Massachusetts sucks?

And, okay. Maybe I'm not the best housekeeper. I'm used to living on my own. I haven't had a boyfriend in years, so who's there to impress?

That's why, when I found the single, solitary rose petal lying flat on my coffee table next to my empty mug, I couldn't understand it.

Where did it come from? What was it doing there?

Vivid red, the edges gone dark as if it was starting to wilt, the lone rose petal stuck out at me. I know it wasn't there when I left for work.

Ten hours later, there it was.

I picked it up, started to throw it away, stopping when I felt a gentle breeze. A touch of sentimentality that I never could've explained kept me from tossing it. Instead, I slipped the rose petal beneath an upside-down glass and pretended it was a keepsake from *Beauty and the Beast* or something.

I don't know.

It wasn't until much later that I remembered the breeze and realized that all of my doors and windows were closed. It was April when I found the petal, still super chilly in Salem, and I needed heat. No way the petal blew in, no explanation for the breeze.

I shrugged and let it go. I didn't think of a ghost then.

Then something really weird happened.

It was the middle of summer, like the beginning of July, when I decided to bake a peach cobbler. And, yeah, so I'm not the world's best baker, either. I like to think of recipes as more like guidelines, and random substitutions and additions are surprises.

Should've remembered that that's not how baking works.

After three hours of peeling peaches, slicing, sautéing, and trying to figure out how to make a crust when I was missing two key ingredients, I ended up with a kitchen that looked like a tornado had blown its way through and a cobbler that managed to somehow be both burned and raw in certain places.

I ate two of the corner pieces anyway before shoving the whole thing in the fridge. Frustrated at the mess, I decided to leave it until the morning.

I regretted it when I woke up, of course, since the gooey peachy mess was stuck to the pan and there was a disaster everywhere I turned.

You think I would have let the dishes soak, right? Nope. I went through two Brillo pads and half a bottle of dish soap to clean it all up.

The dry ingredients were left out, used measuring cups and peach peels everywhere. After the dishes were done, I focused on cleaning up the counters.

At first, I didn't see it. It was only as I was about to wipe up a pile of sugar scattered near the oven that I paused, staring at the spill. I couldn't understand it. It didn't make any sense.

That didn't change what I saw.

Somehow, someway, someone got into my apartment and drew a heart in a pile of spilled sugar. A flippin' heart.

I added a deadbolt to my door that afternoon. Because I might have joked later on to Allison that my apartment was haunted to brush the whole thing off as silly, but I was seriously afraid that a real *alive* person was in my home while I was sleeping.

A ghost I could handle. A creeper? I was gonna protect myself.

Then, in the beginning of September, something so inexplicable happened, I finally gave in and accepted that Casper was here.

I was feeling kinda lonely, a little vulnerable, and—not gonna lie—pretty horny when Jim from accounting asked me out to dinner. Something told me not to do it, but sometimes I let my libido take the lead rather than my brain.

Besides, he was pretty cute.

Handsy, too, I discovered. So maybe it wasn't a brilliant idea to invite him back to my place. He was supposed to drop me off, since the two glasses of wine I had left me feeling a little tipsy and hesitant to drive.

A little loose and relaxed, too. At the entrance to my apartment building, Jim offered to escort me up, and I let him. Then, at my door, I stupidly invited him in.

I realized my mistake about twenty minutes later when we were necking like a couple of kids. I could taste the beer on his breath, feel his hands roaming all over me. And I was into it, too, until he suggested we take our impromptu make-out session into the bedroom.

Now, I like kissing as much as the next woman. But I wasn't about to jump into the sack with a co-worker the first night that we went out. I wasn't even sure that I *liked* Jim all that much. I definitely didn't want to sleep with him.

He definitely didn't want to take no for an answer.

Jim had his hands slipped under my blouse, his body nudging me backwards as if guiding me toward my room. I might've been tipsy, but I still knew what I was doing—and what I wanted.

I started to tell him so and that's when my front door creaked open. An instant later, it slammed shut.

A chilly breeze rushed into the room, tousling his formerly perfectly styled blond hair.

He yanked his hands back as if my bra burned his palms. "I thought you said you lived alone."

"Technically, I do," I told him. Inspiration struck and I added, "I didn't think you'd want to hear about my roommate."

"Roommate?" Jim glanced behind him. "There's no one here, Danielle."

"Of course, there is." I straightened my blouse, careful to keep a bright smile on my face. I wanted to pick up my remote and chuck it at his head. I settled on messing with it instead. "You just can't see him."

"And... and you can?"

"No, silly. Because he's a ghost."

As if on cue, the breeze whooshed through the living room again. I didn't have to look toward the windows to know they were all closed like normal.

I swear, you never saw a man run so fast. Either he believed me when I said it was a ghost—the slamming door finally convinced *me*—or he decided I was nuts. Either way, I never heard from Jim the accounting perv again.

Pity.

Anyway, after that, I decided me and my ghost buddy were friends. Casper must have agreed. The whole aura of the apartment got even homier. Cozier. I might not have really felt alone before, but now it kinda seemed like I had a friend.

The apartment was finally starting to feel like a place I could live in instead of just sleeping in.

It's crazy. I know it sounds absolutely nuts.

But my apartment is definitely haunted.

And I'm surprisingly okay with it.

Zack

I'm in love.

The only problem?

She's alive. And me?

I'm kinda not.

I've got to be a ghost. That's how it works, right? I mean, no one can see me. No one can hear me, either. When I reach out to grab something, my hand goes right through it. I float about eight inches off of the ground.

I don't remember how I died. I... I don't remember much about my life before I was a ghost. I know my first name—*Zackary*—and that's about all.

Oh, and I know that there's no way I can leave the apartment I'm haunting. No matter how many times I try, I can't pass through the front door. Any other door inside? Sure. I can drift out onto the balcony, but there's an invisible wall whenever I try to reach over the decorative railing. I'm stuck here—and I have no idea where *here* is.

It was like, one day I woke up here, and then it seemed like I've always been.

A haze of time, a stretch I can't describe, and then the movers came. Everything that made the apartment feel like a home was taken from me. It might not have been my stuff, but lingering in an empty apartment was my own personal hell.

Lost and alone, I haunted the dark rooms, plotting my escape, endlessly questioning my existence here.

I don't know how long I've been trapped inside. A while, I think. Long enough to know every single inch of the handful of rooms that make up my cage.

I can tell you how many of those tiny tiles are on the bathroom floor—1,693—and where the seams in the shag carpets meet. I know every water stain on the ceiling, the faint cracks in the peeling paint, the empty nail studs that held pictures long gone.

Sometimes I drift in the living room, and imagine what used to hang on the walls. I don't remember, but sometimes I think I can.

I met another ghost once. Lydia. She was an elderly spitfire who claimed the floor above me. In the years since she died, she gathered enough spectral energy—at least, that's what she called it—to move between floors and, sometimes, she would visit me.

She always asked me why I lingered and I could never get the old dear to understand that it wasn't my choice. I didn't want to be here. I always thought that when I dropped dead, that was it. This waiting around in limbo was for the birds.

Especially since I had no idea why I couldn't move on.

Lydia was stubborn enough in life that she refused to move on without her Charlie, she explained. She purposely haunted their place, anxiously waiting until he passed away so they could be together again.

Last Halloween, I guess she got tired of waiting. She told me, ghost to ghost, that Halloween was the one day of the year when the veil between the dead and the living was thin enough to cross over.

And she did.

I remember the scream of holy terror, the blue and red flashing lights, all the people storming the complex. I floated out on the balcony, watching it in morbid curiosity.

And there was Lydia, holding tightly to the hand of her newly deceased husband while waving at me with the other, as the two simply vanished into the black of night.

Whispers through the wall and all around me said it was a heart attack. Yeah. If I was alive and I saw the ghost of my dead wife on Halloween, I might have had a heart attack, too.

Not like I had a wife when I was still kicking. At least, I don't think I did. I don't remember much of when I was still alive. Hell, I don't even know how I died. I just woke up one morning and I was here.

A ghost.

I can't leave, but after Dani moved in, I stopped trying.

Dani.

Ah, Dani.

Can a ghost fall in love with a mortal?

Don't know. Never really thought about it until she came to stay in my apartment and I fell head over heels almost immediately.

She's beautiful. She's kind. She likes to watch comedy sitcoms late at night, and we laugh at all the same cheesy jokes, so her sense of humor is amazing. She talks to herself—I can almost pretend she's talking to me—and she sings with her soul, even if it's terribly off-key. She cries at those sad puppy and kitten commercials, then calls to pledge a donation more often than she probably can afford to.

She reads a lot. Dani's a smart girl.

Mmm. I"m pretty sure I've always had a thing for smart girls.

Oh, and she's got no shame. Her smile makes me think impure thoughts, and her ass... Whoa. Lucky me. Dani's got this habit of walking around naked to dry off after she showers. I learned that one by accident a couple of days after she moved in. For once, I thought I might've found my way to Heaven.

Holy hell, does she have a body that would tempt a saint to sin.

I'm definitely dead. Even an accidental glimpse like that should've been enough to give me a raging cock-stand. Nope. Little Zack didn't so much as even twitch. He's as dead as the rest of my ghostly body.

I'm careful to close my eyes whenever she gets out

of the shower after that. It's not right. Bad enough that she doesn't even know she's sharing her apartment with a dead guy. I refuse to take something from her that she doesn't even know she's giving me.

Even if I really, really want to.

BEST WAY TO UNWIND

Dani

I've just walked out of my apartment and into the hallway when my cell phone rings.

Digging in my purse, my heels *clack* loudly as I scurry toward the steps. Call me a chicken, but I have this thing about elevators. My crazy vivid imagination from when I was a kid left me with a couple of things that make me uncomfortable as an adult.

You see, I have these oddball phobias that most normal people don't.

I'm afraid of tripping and falling into an open grave at the cemetery.

Getting trapped in a pottery kiln and being cremated alive.

Being eaten by a giant lobster.

Walking into an elevator and falling to my death because I didn't notice that the room was missing.

Yeah. My brother used to tease to me, but that never stopped me from being careful. I've made it almost three decades doing things my way, and since I'm still kicking, I figure I'm doing something right.

Besides, I live on the third floor. Running down two flights of stairs because I got a late start isn't me being ridiculous. It's good cardio.

I find the phone at the bottom of my purse just as the ringtone dies. Pulling it out, I see that it was Allison calling. I wonder why. Since it's still before nine, I'm technically not late yet so I doubt she's checking up on me.

Except this is Allison. That's probably exactly what she's doing.

I hit her name, pressing the number for her cell instead of her office line. She answers on the first ring.

"Hey, Dani. Did I wake you?"

Jeez. You oversleep once your first week on the job and your trainer never lets you forget it. It would be easier to hate her if she had an ounce of snottiness in her body. Since she sounds honestly sincere, I shrug it off.

I still roll my eyes, though. "I'm up, and I'm almost at my car. What's up?"

"Two things. You got a sec?"

Now that I've got my phone tucked between my ear

and my shoulder, I use my free hand to start searching my purse for my keys. "Sure."

"I got into the office a little early this morning—"

Of course, she did. This is Allison. I might stay at the office all night because I don't know my limits, but my new pal is up at the crack of dawn every morning. I don't know how she does it.

"—and I thought I would take a peek at the Sanderson account. I found a couple of discrepancies that I thought we could iron out before the holiday. On the first page—"

I'm listening to her. I really am. But I'm also trying to figure out what the hell I did with my keys because they're not in here. I had to have them, though, right? How else did I lock my door?

Wait.

Did I lock my door?

"Ah, crap."

Allison stops in the middle of her report. "Everything okay?"

"Yeah, yeah. Keep going."

She does. And I'm trying really hard to pay attention as I *clack-clack-clack* my way back up the stairs. I grab my door handle and turn. It's not even a little bit locked.

I pull up short when I enter the apartment. My keys are sitting on the floor.

As I ran up the stairs, I remembered that I left them on my bedroom dresser.

Swooping down, I scoop them up and call out, "Thanks, Casper," before leaving my apartment again. I pause only long enough to lock up this time, then I'm running for the stairs again.

Allison's laughter echoes through my phone. "You still making nice with your ghost?"

I'm grinning as I get inside my car. "Screw you. You're just jealous."

"Maybe I am. You at least have Casper. I haven't had a man in my apartment since last Christmas."

"You mean your dad, don't you?" I shake my head, even though she can't see me. "That's sad."

I wasn't in Salem last Christmas and I didn't know Allison then. Since I've met her, she's told me stories about her parents' annual trips into town. The Shaws used to live in Salem, though they live in Florida now. Every Christmas, they come to stay with their daughter and it's always a disaster.

I can't wait to see what happens this year.

Throwing my car into reverse, I press the button on my dash that transfers Allison's call from my cell to the stereo.

"You know," I tell her, grateful that the conversation has gone from a mind-numbing report to something a little bit more juicy, "I can always hook you up with Max. He hasn't given up on his big brother act, even though I'm gonna be thirty soon. I can have him flying cross country in a heartbeat if you're really that desperate. Let him take care of you instead of me for a while."

I mean it, too. I love Max to death but he's been on my ass since I was a kid. With one phone call, I know I can have him on his way to Salem on the next flight. Hell, he's already done it once before. He doesn't think I know, but before I accepted the transfer, he flew out to make sure I'd be happy here.

Sometimes it sucks when your older brother is a partner at the company where you work.

Not that I've ever told Allison—or anyone else in the Salem office—that Max Dennis is my brother. I've purposely used my mother's maiden name as my professional name so that no one could ever accuse me of riding the coattails of my brother's success.

Danielle Williams busted her butt to get where she is. I won't let anyone take that from me.

Still, Max would be a catch. As hard it is to believe, he's an even bigger workaholic than me. I can't tell the last time he had a girlfriend. Allison—with her bubbly personality, crazy work ethic, and killer looks—would be perfect for him.

He's single. She's single. And if I got the two of them together, maybe they would both butt out of my love life and maybe leave the flippin' office once in a while.

Allison just laughs again, as if she doesn't think I'm

serious. "You keep tossing him at me, one of these days I might give in and say yes."

"I'll keep that in mind." I make a mental note to mention Max every chance I get. "I'm on my way now, so I can take a look at the Sanderson report when I get in. What was that other thing you wanted to talk about?"

"Oh, right. I wanted to ask... are you going to the Halloween party tomorrow?"

Me and my big mouth.

I had hoped she'd forget about that. Last week, when I was buried under a mound of paperwork, she took advantage of my distraction and asked me to go to this party one of the other ad managers was throwing. I stupidly said maybe.

"I don't know. Halloween's not really my thing, Allison."

"You have to. It's not often Halloween actually falls on a Saturday *and* a full moon! This party is going to be epic! You simply have to go with me. Okay? You can be my date. We'll have so much fun together."

A Halloween party? That's so not my scene. I'm such a homebody, I swear my couch has ass grooves in it.

I make one last ditch effort to get out of it. "I remember you saying it's supposed to be a costume party. I don't have anything I can wear."

"What if I can find you a costume?"

"Allison, I—"

"No, listen. It doesn't have to be anything fancy. I'm sure I can put something together for you by tomorrow, so long as you promise me that you'll go to the party. Please, Dani? It won't be fun if you don't go."

I should know better. On the other hand, Allison has been nothing but kind and friendly since I moved to Salem. She never asks me for anything.

I sigh in resignation. "Fine."

"Great! Then leave everything to me."

"Nothing slutty," I warn. Allison might have the tits and the super, slender body to pull it off, but if she gives me something revealing, I'll kill her. "I mean it."

Allison's laugh turns evil. "Just trust me, Dani. Maybe after this party, both of our dry spells will be over."

"Allison—"

Click.

Ugh. She hung up on me.

I'm already regretting this.

———

THE SANDERSON ACCOUNT ENDS UP BEING A LOT MORE involved than I thought it would. My morning was taken up with meetings, Allison went out to talk over a proposal with a new client, and by the time we sat down to put our heads together over it, it was afternoon. We worked on it for hours, until Allison started yawning at her desk.

I told her to go home—she'd already put in more than a twelve hour shift—and spent another hour or two fiddling around with the report before all the numbers started to look like squiggles.

That was my cue. Time to get out of there.

Slinking out of the office, my back aching from being hunched all night, I drive home while dreaming of the pint of Ben & Jerry's in my fridge.

It's a Thursday. I don't usually indulge in sweets during the work week, my vain attempt in trying to shed a couple of pounds. Stress always triggers my sweet tooth, though, and after a day like today, I'll be lucky if I don't eat the whole quart in one sitting.

I have a routine. I started it back in college, when classes and midterms and exams used to get the better of me. Monday through Friday, I focus on work. Friday nights through the weekend?

They're mine.

I was never a party girl, but I still knew how to take care of myself. These days, that consists of a hot shower, some cold ice cream, and some fun entertainment. Movies, music, a book... just something to keep my mind off of my stress.

So what if it's Thursday? I deserve a little me time, especially since I'm going to have to give up my Saturday night for that Halloween party.

Even better? When I leave the bathroom after a relaxing shower and waltz naked into my bedroom to look for my robe, I grab my e-reader on the way and notice that a book I've been looking forward to reading has gone live early.

It's already downloaded, waiting for me to dive in.

I can't find my robe and settle on slipping into a clean pair of panties and an oversized t-shirt instead. Based on promises made in the steamy blurb for this sexy romance, it doesn't matter what I put on.

Good chance I won't be wearing either for long.

3

BEETLEJUICE

Zack

I can tell right away that Dani had a hard day at work.

I know everything about her. Trying not to dwell on how much of a stalker that makes me—I console myself with the knowledge that I've been trying to make her aware of my presence for months now—I focus on the way she's hunched over as she lets herself into the apartment.

She immediately kicks off her heels, then reaches up to take her hair out of the loose bun she has it in. The long strands make my ghostly fingers twitch. I'd give anything to touch it.

It looks so damn soft.

I drift behind her as she heads into the kitchen,

veering straight for the fridge. When she grabs the ice cream and sets it on the counter to defrost, I know it was a really tough day. She only ever goes for the Ben & Jerry's when she's stressed.

No surprise, then, when she starts stripping as she leaves the kitchen. When her blouse hits the floor, I pointedly look away. Dani will be showering and—no matter how tempting it is—I refuse to peek.

One of the tricks I've learned since becoming a ghost is zoning out. I'm sure there's a more supernatural term for it. Hell if I know what it is. Lydia never taught me about it, and I've never met another spirit.

I remember the weirdest shit from when I was alive. A lot of it has to do with pop culture. See, there was this Halloween movie I used to watch. Beetlejuice. Unlike what I saw in that movie, there's no handbook for the dead. Learning how to open doors with nothing but my will, nudging rose petals around the house, dragging keys out of the bedroom, they're all skills I had to figure out myself.

Just like zoning out.

Being a ghost is boring. Really boring. I run out of energy too quickly for it to be useful. I can't turn pages and read. Modern technology shorts out if I try to go near it. With Dani working all the time, I let my mind drift off until something catches my attention and brings me back to the real world.

That's usually only whenever Dani returns to the apartment.

Today, though, is different. The ice cream, the shower, the weight on her shoulders—Dani isn't going to be company for me tonight. No sitcoms, no late night TV where she sits snuggled on the couch and I float behind her.

She needs her rest. I zone out and let her have it.

I don't know how long I'm out of it. In the back of my consciousness, I hear the shower turn off and will my eyes closed so that I don't peek at her. The scent of her vanilla shampoo and floral body wash wafts past me and I know she's tucked safely in her room. When she doesn't reappear in the kitchen or the living room, I figure I was right. She must've turned it early.

It's a different scent that catches my attention. Something rich. Chocolaty. Floating into the kitchen, I see that she forgot all about the ice cream she set out on the counter. Condensation beads along the carton, a brown pool of melted chocolate ice cream forming underneath.

I've grown used to Dani's disasters in the kitchen. I think they're adorable, and I've found ways to use some of them to alert her to my presence.

Only, this isn't a mess she made out of frustration. This is forgetfulness.

I like to think I know Dani very well by now. She would never forget her ice cream.

Her bedroom door is open. I take that as an invitation. Technically, as a ghost, I can pass through the door even if it is closed. I often do, when I'm checking on her to make sure she's sleeping all right.

Um. Dani isn't sleeping yet.

The instant I drift in through her open door, I know what caused her to forget all about her ice cream.

My eyesight is fucking great. It might've been that way when I was alive, I'm not sure, but now that I'm dead? I can see everything, even in the dark. My hearing is just as amazing.

So, even though Dani has her dark purple comforter pulled on top of her, I see the furtive motions under the blanket and hear the sounds of her fingers sliding against slick skin.

For the first time since she's lived with me, I just discovered Dani masturbating.

I've never seen anything so hot before in my life— er, death.

I should go. I should shut my ears, spin around, and go. She might joke, call me Casper like she really believes there's a ghost in her apartment, but there's no way my Dani would be happy to know that I could see her in her private moments.

I should go.

I don't.

I *can't*.

Maybe my final resting place will be Hell when I'm done, and I'll probably deserve it.

It'll be worth it, just to have this one moment with her.

I can't help it. My voice is full of anguish and need as I call out to her.

"*Dani.*"

She answers me on a moan. Her hands don't stop working as she says, "Yessss."

I gasp.

Did she... did she hear me?

She answered me like she did.

I try again. "Dani?"

"Mmmm."

She did!

I don't know how or why, but I'm not about to question it. If she can hear me, she can answer me. She knows I'm here. She didn't tell me to go. I can get consent to take this one step further.

Maybe I can—

Well, I don't know. There's not much I can do as a spirit. My hands would float right past her, so I can't actually touch that silky-looking skin or run my fingers through her hair.

My body still hasn't reacted so anything really physical is out.

I never expected to get this far with her. In all my daydreams, I fantasized about picking Dani up and fucking her against the wall. I know that'll never happen. It can't. She's a mortal and I'm a ghost who can't get it up.

It doesn't matter, though. Right now, the way for me to get pleasure is to give my Dani some of her own. And that I think I can do.

But first—

"Dani. I want to make you feel good. Will you let me?"

Dani

"Will you let me?"

His hoarse whisper makes me break out in chills. With a voice like that? I'll let my mystery man do whatever the fuck he wants to me.

This isn't the first time my vivid imagination has run away with me. Half asleep and so horny I won't last a minute playing with myself, I know my dreams have merged with the sexy lumberjack I was reading about before I dozed off.

In the novel, the heroine woke up to find her man willing to go down on her and make her feel amazing.

Should I be surprised that, out of nowhere, I'm fantasizing about some faceless mystery man who wants to do the same to me?

My dream man wants to make me feel good? I like that plan. Lifting my ass off my bed, I shimmy out of my panties. I'm already so turned on, I've soaked through the lace with my juices.

My eyes are still closed. I know this is all in my imagination—nothing but a flippin' amazing fantasy —and I don't want an empty room to cause me to wake up and deal with the sad reality that I'm all alone.

It's bad enough that I'm convinced there's a ghost haunting my apartment. I draw the line at believing he might have manifested tonight in order to help me get off.

Still, if I'm crazy, there's worse delusions out there.

I nod.

His groan carries on the air. "Can I see you?" he asks. "Without the blanket?"

I don't even ask how he knows that I've left the blanket covering me. In my wild thoughts, the gorgeous man who owns such a sexy voice can see in the dark and he's standing at my bedside, watching me finger myself.

And he wants to see more.

Sounds good.

"Okay."

I flip the edge of the blanket away from my stomach, kicking the rest of it off the bed with my feet. My panties are stretched out, wrapped just underneath the bend of my knee. The elastic gives enough that I let my legs fall open.

I hear another groan, deeper this time, then feel the faint tickle on the outside of my thigh.

He blows gently.

The rush of cool air feels so good against my over-heated skin. With another puff, he directs it right on my clit and I go crazy.

"Mmm, yes." Jeez, I'm already panting. Gritting my teeth, I buck my hips up, trying to get the stream right where I want it. "That... whoa, that feels so good."

He blows harder. I want to grab him and pull him closer. Instead, I clutch my sheet between my fingers and yank.

I writhe on my bed, anxious enough to want to escape the overwhelming sensitivity while desperate for more. The coil in my belly is stretched so tight, I feel like I'll shatter the second it breaks.

God, this orgasm is a long time coming. I don't care if this is a dream, or I've finally lost it. In the throes, at this very second, I wouldn't give a shit if a real guy was in here, doing this to me. I'd freak out and call the police after I came, of course, but as I'm chasing the elusive peak, right now I just. Don't. Care.

I'm so close.

"I'm almost there," I grunt, frustrated. "I just need—"

"I know what you need."

The stream of air narrows until all the pressure is

focused directly on my clit. I squirm. It's good—it's *great*—but it's still not enough.

A break in the stream, and then a harsh command.

"Help me help you, Dani. Take your fingers, slip them inside. Fuck yourself with them."

I don't know why I didn't think of that. Probably because I've been waiting for him to do it for me.

I don't know why, considering he's a figment of my horny imagination. If I need stimulation, of course I'm going to have to take care of that myself.

I'm so slick and wet that there's a squishing sound as I reach between my pussy lips and gather moisture. After a second, I realize it's pointless. As soon as I slip my middle finger inside me, I know I'm aroused enough that it'll glide easily.

It's not enough.

I slip in a second finger. It feels a little more full, and the elusive orgasm I'm chasing is suddenly a little more in sight.

"Harder," he rasps.

I pick up the pace. My palm slaps against my pussy. I tilt my hips again so that my clit is hit with every strike.

It's coming—

I'm coming.

"Oh, yes, oh yes, oh… mmm… oh*yes*!"

The coil snaps. Pure pleasure floods me as my toes curl and my thighs shake. It's too much, though, and I slow my rocking, slow my fucking. I want to stop—I don't know how much more I can take—but then he whispers, "Give me more. Just a little bit more, Dani."

So I do.

I ride out the orgasm to the point that it hurts to breathe, and my clit is so swollen, so sensitive that I'm pretty sure I had two or three consecutive climaxes all rolled into one monster one.

I pull my fingers out, wipe them against the front of my tee. My own voice comes out hoarse, like I've been screaming for hours.

"Oh my god. That's was... that was amazing."

"You're amazing."

A sudden breeze whispers against my cheek, soft and gentle and like a sweet kiss goodnight.

My eyes spring open, chest heaving as my hand falls to my side. My t-shirt is bunched all the way up so my boobs are moving up and down as I pant. My blanket is a tangle on the floor.

My panties are MIA.

Reaching out, I feel around for the knob on my bedside lamp. I find it and give it a quick turn.

My bedroom door is open.

There is nobody else in my room.

4

OKAY, THEN

Dani

The next morning, I wake up with a smile on my face and my hand cupping my bare pussy. I have no clue where my panties are. I must have shucked them and tossed them at the height of my wet dream last night.

Mmm. And what a dream.

I haven't had a fantasy like that in ages. A man with a voice like whiskey, whispering to me all the dirty things he wanted to do to me while keeping his hands to himself, watching me like me getting my rocks off is the best thing that's ever happened to him... what woman wouldn't climax from such an erotic dream?

My e-reader is tossed on top of my comforter. Picking it up, I place it on my dresser while making a mental note to buy everything in that author's backlist. She has a gift. Her words mingled with my subconscious and my body's very clear warning signs that it has been too damn long gave me the best orgasm I've had in years.

I feel lighter. Refreshed. I'm almost giddy as I jokingly call out a morning greeting to Casper before hopping into the shower.

It's a good thing he can't answer me. I can only imagine the show I gave my ghost companion last night.

I think about that sometimes. Ever since I accepted that my house is haunted, I wonder about the spirit that lingers here. I don't always sense him—and I'm absolutely certain it's a guy—but, when I do, he makes me feel safe. I imagine him as an elderly gentleman, a kind grandpa who's looking out for a young career woman on her own.

Hopefully Casper went to bed early last night. My orgasms are usually quick. A couple of rubs, a small pop of pleasure, and the tension is released for some time. I can't remember the last time I exploded like I did last night.

It was wonderful.

After my shower, I get dressed. Because I fell asleep so early, I got up way before I usually do. Instead of rushing out the front door, I decide to treat myself to a homemade breakfast instead of a protein bar down at the office.

Going into the kitchen, that's when I see the sunken-in carton of ice cream and the flood of melted chocolate goop that's spread all over my countertop.

I feel my cheeks heat up. What a flippin' idiot. I can't believe I let a whole carton of Ben & Jerry's go to waste because I was too busy playing with myself.

I grab the carton and toss it in the trash. Wiping down the melted ice cream off the counter doesn't take too long. Before I know it, I've had my breakfast, slipped into my heels, and grabbed my purse.

Look at me. I even know where my keys are.

Hmm. For once, maybe I'll even beat Allison into the office.

———

TODAY GOES MUCH EASIER THAN YESTERDAY.

The minor flaw in the Sanderson report seems so simple now. I'm able to make the corrections, contact the clients, and start on a new project all before lunch. I grab a quick bite to eat with Allison, changing the subject when she casually mentions that tomorrow is Halloween.

As if I forgot. Yeah, right. You can't forget that it's Halloween in Salem. Not with the decorations, the tourists, the hoopla surrounding the holiday. I'll be glad when it's November.

I almost think I managed to dodge the Halloween party bullet entirely when Allison insists I accompany her to her car at the end of her shift. She opens her trunk and pulls out a large shopping bag and tells me not to look inside of it.

"What is it?"

"Your costume for tomorrow. What? You didn't think I'd forget, did you?"

I didn't think so. I just hoped she had.

"Try it on when you get home," she instructs. "It's not too much, and I'm sure you're gonna look great, but I want you to let me know how it fits. I can always come up with something else if you don't like it. Just give it a chance first, okay?"

Since I've already accepted that there's no getting out of this, I nod and take the stupid bag. I don't flip her the bird until she's halfway out of the lot. I'm pretty sure she saw me, considering I can see her shoulders shaking as if she's laughing before she pulls away.

Even though I got a lot of work done today, I still have to stay late. As much as I look forward to my weekends, I won't enjoy myself or unwind if I leave anything left undone at work. I'm at my desk straight through dinner, then end up on a two-hour conference call with Max and some of the other partners.

Sometimes I wonder if he forgets about the three-hour time difference between Massachusetts and California. By the time I get off the phone, it's ten o'clock here. Max still being at work until past seven is normal for him. Me getting stuck downtown this late? On the Friday night before Halloween?

I'm lucky to make it back to my building by eleven, and that's only because I stopped by a drive-thru on the way home so I didn't have to cook when I dragged myself back up the stairs.

I've got the last of my soda in one hand, my purse slung over my shoulder, and Allison's bag bouncing off each step as I trudge my way up to the third floor.

Whoops. Hope she didn't pack anything breakable.

Letting myself into my apartment, I drop my purse on my couch and toss my keys on top of it. I set my drink on the coffee table. For a second, I think about looking for a coaster before shaking my head. A little water never killed anyone.

I'm pooped. My high from this morning is long gone. All I want to do is wash my face, change into a cozy pair of pajamas, and climb into bed.

Then I remember the heft of the bag in my hand and sigh.

Allison made me promise to try it on. If I don't do it now, there's a good chance I won't do it until it's time to leave and then I can only imagine what I'll be stuck with. Better to be safe than sorry.

Tossing the bag onto the couch, I shrug off my coat

then swap it for whatever Allison has packed up for me. The first thing I pull out of the bag is a slinky black dress that I really hope has some spandex in it otherwise I've got no idea how I'm gonna get it on over my head and, well, other body parts.

There's only one other thing in the shopping bag. It's black, like the dress, and I'm not sure what it's supposed to be until I grab it and give it a shake. A pointed top pops up, while a circular bottom is revealed.

I chuckle under my breath. It's a stereotypical witch's hat.

For my first Halloween in Salem, Allison has me dressed up as a witch.

Well, I did tell her I wanted it simple.

I add the hat to the pile growing on the edge of my couch. I'm not worried about that fitting. Nope. I'm still questioning the scrap of fabric Allison considers a dress.

Here goes nothing.

There's no point in going into my bedroom to change. Standing in my living room, I quickly strip down to my bra and panties, then try to figure out how to get this thing on.

It's easier than I first thought. The material has a good amount of give to it. Thank God. I tug on the dress, grateful that it's closer to something Morticia Addams would wear than some of the skimpy costumes I'm used to seeing marketed toward adult women. My boobs are secure and the dress goes down to my ankles. Sure, it's tight, and it leaves nothing to the imagination, but at least I'm not gonna freeze.

You know what? I'll take it.

Anyway, it's just one night. And it'll make Allison happy.

My mind made up, I start to slip the dress off of my shoulders so that I can shimmy it down my body when, out of nowhere, I hear it.

Crash.

I jump and spin around.

Behind me, on the floor, is a vase my mother gave me as a housewarming gift. It was the ugliest damn thing I've ever seen and now that it's smashed into twenty different pieces on my floor, it doesn't look any better.

Only one problem.

I wasn't anywhere near the table.

So how did it fall?

Zack

Dani's vase is smashed to bits on the floor.

I did that.

I... I'm not sure how.

I know *why*. The sight of her luscious body poured into that tight black dress gave me a shock. I felt a quiver down below, the first twitch in ages, and the surprise had me jolt backwards. Slamming into the side table, I knocked into the vase perched on top.

I broke it.

And I wasn't using any spectral energy at all. I wasn't even really *here* at all. After blowing through all my reserves last night with Dani in her bedroom, I needed a good rest and recharge period. So I was zoning out, replenishing my energy, when something called my consciousness back to the apartment.

Finding myself in the living room, I tried to focus on what called me back. That's when I saw Dani wearing that heart-stopping dress. And since I was standing behind her? I got the best view.

Little Zack approved.

Little Zack wasn't supposed to get an opinion any longer.

I jumped back when I felt the twitch. My back hit the table and *boom*. There went that ugly ass vase.

That shouldn't have happened, either. I should've floated right through the table, not bump into it and send her decorations flying.

What the hell is going on here?

I look at my hands.

Is it just me, or do they look a little more... substantial than normal?

Something's happening. Something I can't explain.

Something that's causing me to freak the fuck out.

I drift away from Dani and out onto the balcony just to prove I can. As if I'm made of smoke, I go through easily, only to stumble when I head outside. My feet land hard on the balcony floor. For the first time that I can remember, I'm not floating.

My heart starts to thud. The moon is full, big and round and vaguely yellow over my head.

Underneath the moonlight, my body shudders. Another jolt. I stare.

I can't see through my hands any longer. My arms? Completely solid.

Rushing forward, I place my hands against the sliding glass and push. The barrier is absolute. The cool glass meets the tips of my fingers and stops me from going inside. Slightly panicking, I reach for the edge and tug.

No dice.

I'm locked out on the balcony.

I know every inch of this place. I know that there's no way that I can get down from the balcony without vaulting over the side and breaking my brand new corporeal body. Since I have no clue how I managed to get one back, there's no way I want to risk anything happening to it.

That leaves me one choice.

Taking a deep breath—*whoa*, it feels so weird to actually breathe in air again—I fold my hand into a fist.

Dani

I'm just cleaning up the rest of the broken vase when I hear it.

Rap, tap, tap.

My back goes stiff at the sound. I slowly straighten, holding out my brush and dust plan as if they'll protect me.

What was that?

Rap, tap, tap.

Is that knocking?

Rap, rap, rap, TAP.

Okay. So that *is* knocking. Impatient knocking. But it's not coming from my front door. Unless I'm way off, the insistent tapping is coming from my balcony.

How?

Setting the dustpan and brush on the coffee table, I grab my phone and edge closer to the sliding door that leads out to the balcony. I have gauzy curtains that keep people from seeing too much of my apartment, but still let me see what's outside.

A silhouette of a man is out there. On my balcony.

On the night before Halloween.

Oh, hell no.

"I don't know how you got up here, but you better find a way back down before I call the cops." I brandish my cell phone at him. "I'll give you to the count of three and you better be gone."

The silhouette moves. I edge even closer.

"You're still standing there," I hiss. My heart is beating a mile a minute. "One—"

"Dani, please."

My hand tightens on my phone.

He... he knows my name. How does he know my name?

I press the 9 with my thumb.

"Two—"

"You don't understand. I live here, too."

That makes me pause. Maybe... maybe this isn't as nefarious as I first guessed. Maybe this is a case of mistaken identity. Like this guy thinks this is his apartment—or his girlfriend's maybe—and he found his way to my balcony instead. Maybe we're neighbors and that's how he knows my name.

Damn it. He sounds so earnest. So kind. But Ted Bundy did, too, I remember.

"Bullshit. This is my apartment. I've been here for almost ten months and I don't have a roommate."

"Listen to me, Dani. I... I can explain."

There's no humor in my laugh. He can explain? I highly doubt that.

The balcony goes dark. I spare a quick flicker up at the sky. A massive black cloud has drifted in front of the moon, bathing the balcony and the stranger perched on it in shadow.

I glance back at him, then do a double-take. Tiptoeing toward the door, I yank the gauzy curtain back so that nothing interferes with my sight. Then, careful not to drop my phone, I rub both of my eyes 'cause there's no way in hell that I'm seeing what I think I'm seeing.

He's... he's see-through.

Seriously. There's a faint outline where I know this wacko is still standing there, but beyond that? I can see the building behind him while looking right *through* him.

"What..." It comes out strangled. I swallow the sudden lump in my throat, my heart going thump-thump-thump as I just about whisper, "what's going on here?"

Still half visible, the man on my balcony moves closer to the sliding door. With a curious look on his handsome face, he presses against the glass—except he doesn't actually have to press. There's no resistance. He floats right through the damn door.

And, suddenly, he's in my apartment with me.

This *ghost* is in my apartment with me.

Okay, then.

Taking a deep breath, I let loose the loudest scream I can.

5

LET ME IN

Zack

W ell.

That could have gone over better.

Dani has stopped screaming, though I get the idea that it's not because she's suddenly decided that she's okay with a strange man invading her space, but more like she's ran out of breath.

When she takes in another lungful of air and opens her mouth as if to let loose another shriek, I hurriedly wave my hands to try and stop her.

Shit. What if another neighbor thinks she's being murdered in here? Calls the cops?

No fucking way.

Can you imagine?

Hello, officer. What's going on? Well, you're never gonna believe it—

And they won't. But that's not even the worst part. More than anything, I just don't want Dani to be afraid of me.

"Don't scream again," I hurriedly plead. "Ah, jeez, I'm sorry. I didn't mean to scare you. Look, if it makes you feel better, I'll go back outside. How's that sound?"

Here's hoping I can.

To be honest, I don't have a fucking clue what the hell's going on.

One second, I'm a ghost. A spirit. Nothing, really.

The next? I've got a mortal body again.

Considering what just happened, I have a sneaky suspicion that it's got something to do with the moon. The second the clouds covered it, I went ghost again.

I glance over my shoulder. The clouds have filled the sky, darkening the balcony. My hands are still partially see-through.

Before I think better of it—before I upset Dani even more—I push past the sliding door again. It gives me a little resistance and a peek skyward reveals a sliver of the big harvest moon.

Okay then. It definitely has something to do with the moon.

Once I'm safely outside again, Dani starts pacing in front of the door. Like a gentleman, I try my hardest to stare straight ahead because, otherwise, my eyes will

46

be glued to the gorgeous sway of her ass. Not the best way to endear me to her, I'm betting.

And then she says, "This... this is a joke. It's gotta be. A Halloween prank, that's it."

My stomach sinks. Halloween? Already?

Ever since Dani moved into the apartment, I lost track of the individual days. My mornings and nights begin and end with her smile and her sighs, her laughs and the twinkle in her brilliant blue eyes. A ghost has no use for hours, minutes, days.

But Halloween.

Hell.

That explains it.

I should've known when I gathered enough energy to pleasure her last night. I thought it was because I wanted Dani so bad, that I was finally able to slip into her consciousness and make her hear me, feel me. It had never happened before—and I've been trying to seduce my living houseguest for months— and I figured I've finally tapped into some new ghost power.

I guess I did. And the magic of Halloween lent it to me.

So Lydia was right.

"Listen, I'm sure I can explain this all properly if you just give me the chance. Okay? Open the door, I'll come inside, and we can discuss this like rational adults."

"You're a ghost," she snaps. "Why are you asking me? Just float back in if you want."

I try. With the moon shining bright again, I try to float back in—but I can't. I'm as solid and human as she is. The glass door keeps me out.

I see another bank of clouds moving quickly across the sky. I decide to wait until it covers the moon again. If my theory is right, I should be able to go back inside and explain this—somehow—to Dani.

The moon dims, the clouds filling the sky. I squint at my hands.

Shit.

They look kind of solid still.

I try to press against the glass again. It doesn't work.

And then it finally hits me.

What time is it? It must be after midnight. It's *Halloween* Halloween, a full moon looming over my head. And I'm fucking human again.

Wait.

If I'm human, then that means—

"Dani." I'm suddenly pleading. I don't care. I'm desperate. To be near her, to feel her, to touch her. Because I'm human and I *can*... if she'll let me. "Let me in."

She freezes. "Say that again."

"Let me in."

Suddenly, she's flushing. Red floods her cheeks,

making her look more embarrassed than angry. After hesitating, she opens the sliding door by a crack.

I don't know what made Dani change her mind, but I slip awkwardly through the small gap before she changes it again and shoves me back onto the balcony.

"Thanks."

"I know your voice. How do I know your voice?"

Her deadly whisper causes shivers up and down my spine. Dani is a head shorter than me, fifty pounds lighter, and up until five minutes ago, I was a full-fledged ghost. She witnessed me passing through her glass door.

Then why am I the one who's terrified now?

"Umm..."

She screws up her face, as if trying hard to place the sound of my voice. It probably doesn't help that I said something really close to that when I was pleading with her last night. If the memory of what happened in her bedroom is seared as powerfully in her mind as it is mine, it won't take her long to remember.

I know the instant it does.

Her hands fold into fists. "It's you."

"Dani, I—"

"Don't deny it. You were there last night. You were there last night while I... and I never saw you."

I can't deny it. I wouldn't if I could.

Instead, I say, "You were right before. I *am* a ghost."

Dani

He's... he's a ghost.

My second thought? I let a ghost go down on me.

My third?

"What kind a perv ghost takes advantage of the women living in his haunted house?"

"What?"

"You heard me!" Totally ignoring the fact that I was into everything he did to me when I thought it was just me fantasizing an imaginary lover, I stamp my foot and glare up at him. Fear gives way to fury. He's gorgeous, okay, but that won't save him. "Is that how you get your kicks? Seducing lonely women?"

He looks offended. "Dani, you've got the wrong idea. I... I wasn't trying to seduce you."

"You might not have been trying, but you damn well did."

I know this isn't the right time to have this argument. First of all, he's a ghost who isn't a ghost anymore all of a sudden. He's also a ghost who believes he lives here with me. And, well, he's also a ghost who gave me oral last night.

And I *let* him.

"I didn't mean for any of that to happen, but I won't say that I didn't want it to. I only wanted to alert you to your melting ice cream. Then, when I saw what you were doing—I couldn't help myself.

You were too beautiful. I wanted to make you feel good."

This is such a bizarre conversation. I should be kicking him out of my place, maybe running to get myself committed, not talking about my night-time fingering and the part he had to play in it.

I can't help it, though. Even if he just appeared, I kind of feel like I know him already. And the Casper I knew is nothing like the flippin' hunk standing in front of me.

This has to be Casper, though. The safe feeling I got from my ghost is here in this room right now and it's coming from him. As soon as I kinda recognized him, my fear was short-lived anyway. He knows my name. He knows about the ice cream.

He knows about what I did under my blanket, and how he offered to help.

How he *did* help.

This handsome guy *is* my Casper and that realization makes me feel vulnerable. Vulnerable and a little testy.

Hands on my hips, I raise my eyebrows over at him. "How many other women bought that line?"

"None."

"And you think I'm naive enough to? Gee, Casper. Thanks."

He shakes his head. "You misunderstand me."

"Oh, no. I think I'm understanding you just fine."

"There hasn't been any other women."

Wait.

What?

I squint my eyes, getting him entirely in focus. Now that he's inside my—well, I guess, *our*—apartment, he's filled out some. I can't see through him at all any more. But what I do see? He's absolutely yummy for a formerly dead guy.

Yeah, right. Like I believe that there hasn't been any other women.

"You don't have to give me that baloney. You already saw me naked."

"It's not baloney, Dani," he insists. "You're the only one I've every appeared for—the only one I ever wanted to do that to." His dark eyes gleam as he takes a step toward me. "I love you."

OKAY. WE'VE GOTTA BACK UP A LITTLE.

Somewhere, some way, I lost control of this conversation. All I wanted to do was figure out where I knew that voice from. How did that escalate to me actually letting him into my apartment?

How did that lead to him telling him he loves me?

Pushing past that totally unexpected admission, I shake my head. "Okay. Okay. Say I believe this. Say I accept that you're the Casper who's been haunting my place. We've gotta start at the beginning. All right?"

"Whatever you want, Dani."

I want him to stop using my name. Every time he does, I get a tingle in a very inappropriate place.

Instead, I gesture at my couch. The indication is clear. He needs to sit.

He does. I stay standing, feeling a little more in control.

"First: who *are* you?"

"My name is Zackary."

"No last name?"

His face shadows over. "Not that I can remember."

Okay then. "How long have you been here? In this apartment, I mean."

"I don't know. A while. I was here way before you moved in."

"When did you die?

He shifts in his seat. My questions are obviously making him uncomfortable, just like his lack of answers are bothering me. I'm not surprised when he says, "I don't know.

No name. No time frame. There's no way for me to look him up, or discover if he's telling the truth. One thing for sure: he's definitely a ghost. Or he was. I'm kind of hazy on that point.

But if he was a ghost, that means he died.

There's probably some kind of protocol when it

comes down to interrogating a phantom on Halloween. I'm willing to bet that asking how they became a ghost in the first place is against some kind of etiquette.

That doesn't stop me.

"Zackary—"

"Zack," he murmurs. "Call me Zack. Please."

Sure. "Zack, *how* did you die?"

He lowers his gaze, staring at the hands in his lap.

"I... I don't know."

He looks so lost, so confused that I don't push it. "You said you live here, too. Can you leave?"

His whole expression changes in an instant. "It's Halloween, the one night of the year that I can cross over and be human. All I've wanted since you moved in here was to have a moment like this, where we could talk. Are you asking me to go?"

He'd go if I told him so. I know that as certainly as I do that everything that is happening right now is flippin' nuts.

He was a ghost, but now that it's gonna be Halloween, he isn't now.

I should kick him out. This is absolutely crazy. At the same time, though, I have to admit that— once my initial shock wore off—I'm really curious about everything that's going on.

I shake my head. "I just wanted to know."

"I think I can leave the apartment now, but to

answer your question: no. Up until tonight, I couldn't go."

My emotions are all over the place. Curiosity turns to surprise to horror in a heartbeat.

Maybe Casper is a perv ghost after all.

"So you're always here? When I'm sleeping? When I shower?" When I'm *naked*?

Zack hesitates, then nods.

I don't say anything else at first. I'm not even thinking about last night. This is all about the last ten months.

Because this is Casper, I'm trying really hard to get past the fact that he can go in my bedroom—my *bathroom*—whenever he wants. It never really occurred to me before. What if—does he *spy* on me?

He must read how uncomfortable and angry and really, really confused I am because he's up and pacing all of a sudden, like we've traded places. He runs his hands through his thick, shaggy hair, obviously agitated, while a pair of wild, dark brown eyes search for me every time he swings back around.

"I know what you're thinking, Dani, and it's not like that. I didn't peek, I swear, I never peeked."

Oh, yeah? I quirk an eyebrow. "Really? Then what do you call what happened in my bedroom last night?"

Twin spots of color rise up on his cheeks. "I'd call it magical, but I know that's not what you mean."

The look he gives me, the heated rasp in his deep

tone, it makes me quiver. He called my orgasm magical.

He's not wrong.

I just thought that I was the only one who believed that.

6

CASPER THE FRIENDLY GHOST

Zack

D ani goes quiet. I don't know if it's a good thing or a bad thing that she's given up on her interrogation for a moment.

Huh. Some interrogation. I could barely answer any of her questions.

I wish I knew more. I wish I could tell her more.

I'm so keyed up. I'm not used to all this energy. Pacing helps. I walk the length of her living room, back and forth, waiting to see what her next move is going to be.

Surprisingly, it's not my ex-ghost status that seems to bother her. She doesn't even seem too put out that I really *am* a ghost, or that some kind of Halloween magic has allowed me to materialize in front of her at last. I was afraid the truth about last night might be the nail in my figurative coffin.

Nope.

It's the idea that I might've spent the last ten months peeking. After the lengths I went to to avoid doing so, it doesn't seem fair that that's the sticking point.

I want to explain myself. If only I could find the words.

And that's when, on another loop, I see it. The upside down glass.

She still has it.

Without a word, I walk over to it and look at the glass. Underneath it, I see the rose petal I left for her.

My heart swells. Thank goodness, right now, it's the only body part to do so. "I'm so glad you kept my gift."

Her voice is soft. Quiet. "Your gift?"

I nod. "You wouldn't believe how long it took me to get it for you."

It was my first big use of spectral energy. I was tapped out for over a week, but it was worth it the first time I saw the glass protecting it. All these months later, it's still here.

And that makes me think that maybe I have a chance.

I just can't screw this up again. Not yet. Not when I still have a whole day left to show her how much I care.

How much I fucking *want* her.

I glance over at Dani. She's watching me with a very curious look.

"What?" I ask. I'm careful to keep my voice light, a non-threatening smile on my face.

She thinks I'm Casper. Okay. Friendly ghost it is.

Dani flushes. "But... but *why*?"

"Lots of reasons. I mean, first off, a guy ought to bring flowers to a girl if he wants her to know he's serious. And, well, I am serious. I wasn't kidding when I said I love you."

She turns away from the intensity of my gaze. As if the broken vase we both forgot about is suddenly the most important thing in the world, she turns instead toward the brush and pan she abandoned on her coffee table.

I don't blame her. Dani clearly doesn't want to hear about my feelings for her. If I was alive, I would respect that—but I'm living on borrowed time. It's already half past twelve which means I'm already down thirty minutes.

But how to make her understand all of this? That I was dead, but now I'm not, but I will be again tomorrow?

She bends over and I get my first big clue that, no matter how it happened—spectral energy, Halloween magic, a fucking birthday wish, I don't know—I'm really, truly alive at this moment.

My blood races straight to my groin. My cock twitches and immediately starts to swell. My eyes are glued to Dani's ass, the lush curves, the taut globes outlined enticingly against her dress. I suddenly can't get the sight out of my head, or stop wondering how it would cushion her once I impaled her on my cock and let her ride.

The image has me ready to spill in my pants. There's already a pretty big tent in front. Dani gets an eyeful of that, she might just start threatening me with the cops again.

As she straightens and starts to turn, I panic and reach for one of the decorative throw pillows. I manage to cover my crotch in time for her to look back at me.

Did I think that would hide it?

The way her eyes dip down, her lips curling as she sees the floral-printed pillow pressed tightly to my aching cock... Dani snorts. I'm not fooling her at all.

I hold my breath. It still feels really weird, though all of my attention is on my pulsing hard-on and my sudden fear that she's going to kick me out of the apartment for real.

Dani shakes her head, that long brown hair swaying with the motion.

"You know that? I'm too tired for this. I've been up all day, working hard. It's Friday and I want to go to bed. We can figure it out in the morning."

We. She said we. I exhale a shaky breath. "Okay," I agree. "Tomorrow."

"Since you're human now, you need to get some sleep." All of my high hopes and dirty fantasies die a sudden death when she looks pointedly at her sofa. "You sleep there."

It's not her bed, but I'll take it.

I DON'T SLEEP, THOUGH.

I can't. I'm too excited, and since my achingly hard cock agrees with me, it's almost impossible to sleep. How can I? When I know that the love of my afterlife is sleeping just beyond that obviously locked door?

One downside to rematerializing: now that it's officially Halloween, I can't go ghost. I tried. Nope. Human again. Even if I let my lusts rule me, there's no way for me to slip past that barrier.

Dani wants me on her sofa. I just want to watch her sleep, maybe hear her breathe—and, okay, she kinda snores. I want to hear her snore, watch her toss and turn all night. I love her quirks because I love her. And I love her enough to respect her wishes.

I'm not a complete idiot. I know how close I came to being tossed out on the curb. She didn't have to let me stay here, and I pride myself on the orgasm I gave her.

It definitely affected her, which means she might be willing to do it again.

And I'll be ready when she is.

Dani

I barely sleep a wink. When I finally drag myself out of my bed and go to confront my new houseguest—and, I don't know, roommate?—I find that he couldn't have slept at all.

The whole place flippin' sparkles. That's the only word for it. My glass coffee table gleams. All of the furniture has been polished, leaving a hint of lemon Pledge in the air. I left all of my crap on my couch and that's gone. I see my purse hanging off the front door knob, the witch's hat and costume folded neatly on my dinner table.

Pledge isn't the only thing I smell. As I follow my grumbling stomach into the kitchen, I find Zack at the stove. He's got a spatula in one hand, tending to something in the pan. I take another tentative sniff, just in case I'm imagining it.

Nope. I smell blueberries.

"Morning, sleepyhead. I've been waiting for you to get up."

He's too cheery. I'm immediately suspicious. "Good morning. I see you're still here."

"Yup. And I'm still human, too. For a little bit longer, at least."

"You're in a good mood," I point out.

Zack glances over his shoulder. He throws a grin my way and, for a second, I stop breathing. I remember thinking last night that he was good-looking. In the light of day, while he's cooking in my kitchen, I decide he might be the most gorgeous man I've ever seen in my life.

Of course. Leave it to me to to be attracted to a ghost.

"I'm in a great mood," he tells me, turning back to flip his pancake. "Why wouldn't I be? It's All Hallow's Eve. Halloween. I was able to get my body back, if only for just today, and you were kind enough to take a chance on me."

That's a nice way of saying that I could've thrown his ass out of the apartment last night and didn't.

I'm still not sure why. I mean, yeah, for the last couple of months I've gotten used to the idea that my apartment came with a ghost. Some places came with furniture, some appliances, and mine had a spirit attached. Fine. Whatever.

He wasn't supposed to show up as a six foot tall, dark-haired, scruffy Adonis of a man who, within minutes of being able to speak to me, tells me that he loves me.

Because that part? I remember it vividly.

And, I admit to myself, it's why I had to take the chance.

I shake my head. "Forget about it. It's just one day, right? Then you go back to being Casper?"

I see Zack's shoulders tighten as he hunches over my stovetop. "Halloween is the only time a ghost can cross over," he says, "so yes. When midnight comes, I'll most likely be gone."

Oof.

The conversation dies a slow death then and there. I don't know what else to say, and Zack busies himself with his cooking. It's fascinating how well he navigates my kitchen, as if he knows every inch of it.

Duh, Dani. Considering he maybe, kind of, sort of lives here too, he probably does.

Wonderful.

He reaches into the cabinet above the stove, pulling out a plate. Using the spatula, Zack takes three fluffy pancakes from the stack and slides them onto the plate. A tab of butter on top, followed by so much syrup my pancakes are swimming in it.

Instead of giving me the plate, he takes it out of the kitchen and sets it on the dining room table. He pulls a chair out and gestures for me to take a seat.

"For you, Dani."

Blueberry pancakes smothered in butter and syrup.

Taking the offered seat, I murmur, "Thank you. They're my favorite."

"I know."

The way he says that so matter-of-fact should be creepy. I don't know what it says about me that I'm touched instead.

And then I think about him touching me and yeah. I quickly pick up a forkful of pancakes and shove it into my mouth before I say something I really shouldn't.

AFTER BREAKFAST, I TELL HIM I'M GOING TO TAKE A shower. I only give Zack one warning that he better not peek before I lock the door behind me and jump in.

Part of me wonders what the hell I'm doing. I only met this man less than twelve hours ago and I'm trusting him not to break down the door while I'm wet and soapy and naked. How would I be able to defend myself?

I wouldn't.

But that's the thing. I'm not afraid of Zack. I know it sounds crazy. This whole flippin' thing is certifiably crazy. Then again, how big a leap is it from accepting that ghosts exist to finding out one can pop up on Halloween?

I saw *Casper* when I was a kid. That's like the whole

plot of the movie. Shoot, maybe I was onto something there when I first gave him a name.

By the time I'm dressed and ready to confront the reality of today, I discover that he put away the leftover pancakes I hadn't managed to gobble up, cleaned up the kitchen, washed the dishes, and returned them to their proper place.

I feel terrible. I don't want him to think that I let him stay because I wanted a manservant or something. For all I know, he's been dead for years and I'm wasting his one day by allowing him to wait on me.

"You didn't have to do that."

"Do what?"

Why does he look so damn hot when he's puzzled? A lock of dark hair falls forward, barely kissing his eyes as his nose scrunches up. It's not fair.

I wave my hand toward the kitchen. "Breakfast. Cleaning up my apartment. All of it."

"Oh. I know. I just wanted to do a little something to show you how much I care."

Right. Because he loves me.

I wish I could believe that. Who wouldn't want a man who looks like he does *and* can make a pancake that fluffy?

I thought about that last night, too. He only thinks he loves me because I'm the one who moved into his apartment.

Shame, but it's got to be true. I mean, it's not like he'd pick me if he had a choice.

At least there's one thing he has a choice about right now.

"Yeah. Anyway, I'm sure you have much better things to do today than help me do my chores. It's the only day you get to be human, right? You said something last night about being able to leave the building now. You should really get out, make the most of your time."

Zack frowns and just the one look creates a pang that hits me straight in the heart. He looks crushed. "Now that it's morning, you want me to go?"

"Don't *you* want to go?"

"Um, no. Not even a little. Sorry. I don't have the time to waste so I'm being more forward than I normally would. Hope you don't mind."

I don't. I probably should, and I don't.

"It's all right. You can stay here if you want. I'm not doing anything today, either, so if you hang around, you'll have to deal with me."

"Really? Promise?"

I laugh. He sounds so eager. Poor Casper. He must be so lonely. "Okay. So we're staying in. It's still your day. What do you want to do?"

And then he says the last thing I ever would expect—

"We should watch all of the Halloween Heist episodes from Brooklyn Nine-Nine."

My mouth drops open. He looks like that, makes a killer blueberry pancake, is convinced I'm awesome *and* wants to watch my favorite show?

Oh, boy.

I'm in trouble.

———

From my questions last night, it's clear there's not much he remembers from when he was alive. I'm stubbornly trying to pretend that he hasn't been invisible in my home these last ten months, learning all my secrets.

So we do what any two strangers do when they meet and feel that undeniable spark. We hang out and get to know each other while lounging about on my couch.

I already know that we share the same taste in television. And, okay, it's obvious that Zack only found out about these shows because they're the ones I watch when I'm unwinding from work, but that doesn't mean he has to like them. From his deep laugh and the way he does an amazingly deadpan Holt impersonation, I can tell he enjoys them almost as much as I enjoy watching him watch it.

It takes a couple of hours to get through five half-hour episodes because we both keep finding reasons to pause the show. A throwaway comment from one of the characters might lead to an intense discussion or maybe a what-if scenario that we talk out.

In the back of my mind, bonding with a ghost over Brooklyn Nine-Nine turns into a first date with Zack. When we get to the big proposal scene in HalloVeen, my emotions get the better of me and I start focusing on what his lips look like instead of what he's saying.

They're kind of soft and pillowy-looking and it isn't long before I wonder if I should kiss him.

He'd let me. I know he would.

But I don't. I'm already dangerously close to falling for my ghost. Making it physical would be a mistake.

Even though the other night proves that the spark between us can be mighty combustible.

When our show is done, I offer to take Zack out for lunch. His hesitation leads me to order a pizza in for us. It's a treat, because I rarely splurge on pizza since I'm one person and I hate leftovers. But with two of us, I order a large, and I'm not even a little surprised when Zack tells me that his favorite toppings are pepperoni and mushrooms.

They're mine, too. Damn it.

He didn't eat any of breakfast and I started to think that, since he's a ghost, he didn't have to. Then the pizza arrives and he puts away four slices by the time I finish two. He even asks me for my crust when I'm not quick enough to finish it. I point out that, if he was hungry, he should've had some breakfast.

With a sheepish grin, Zack admits that he doesn't like blueberries or pancakes. Well, he couldn't be *perfect*. He gets points for making me a breakfast he would never eat.

So not perfect, but pretty damn close.

Too bad he's dead.

IN THE MIDDLE OF THE LATEST HALLOWEEN SPECIAL we're watching, my phone starts buzzing. When it keeps going and I don't reach for it, Zack strokes the top of my foot. He's been doing that more and more as the afternoon wore on—finding reasons to touch me, small caresses that seem sweet instead of pervy—and the heat from his fingertip leaves a tingle against my skin that makes me want more.

"Dani?"

"Mmm."

"Shouldn't you answer that?"

I... I don't want to, I realize. The ring has ripped me right out of this cozy moment. I don't want to answer my phone. I want to fling it into my bedroom and forget that it exits.

I've been living a daydream today, letting myself get more and more attached to a man who's going to disappear at midnight tonight. There's something about Zack. It's too easy. I feel so comfortable around him, like I've known him forever instead of a couple of hours.

Well, I guess I've known him for months if I think of him as Casper, but still.

The phone stops ringing. I let out small sigh of relief that's short-lived. A minute after the phone goes silent, the ring starts up again.

Rising up off of the couch, I grab for the phone I left sitting on the coffee table. I see Allison's picture on the front of the screen and groan.

It all comes back to me in a rush. "It's Allison. I bet she's calling about the party. Ugh. I can't believe I forgot all about the party."

"Party?"

"Office costume party. For Halloween? It's why I was trying that skimpy dress on last night. Allison got it for me so that I can go to this party."

Zack chuckles. "Then you have to thank Allison for me. Seeing you in that dress was a revelation. You've gotta go tonight if only so I can see you wearing it again."

Feeling my cheeks heat up at his husky voice, I reach over and smack Zack with a couch pillow.

He pretends to dodge it, grinning when I manage to hit him right in the thigh. "In all seriousness, you promised your friend you'd go, right?"

I plop down on the couch and rest my weapon in my lap. I set my phone on top of it. The ring dies again but I know it won't last. Allison can be determined like that.

"I did."

"Then you should go."

"Zack—"

"And since I won't waste any of the time I have with you, I'll just have to go, too."

I... Wow. I kind of like that idea. I mean, I was having fun hanging out with Casper—with Zack. This party Allison wants me to go to promises to suck. I think it'll suck less if I bring my ghost friend with me.

Only one problem.

"It's a costume party. I'm set, but what will you go as?" I ask him.

7

DANI'S CLOSE FRIEND

Zack

I don't let Dani out of my sight.

A lot of my life before becoming a ghost is a blur. Parties, though... I think I remember parties. They weren't anything like this.

On the way over, Dani explained that this was a get together for the people who work in her office. I imagined a small gathering, maybe a handful of others. I don't know how many people work out of her office because there's got to be like a hundred partygoers here.

The music is loud. The lights are low. A live band—ironically dressed as skeletons—play music on a stage. Strings of orange lights criss-cross the low ceiling.

Pumpkins and hay bales and half-dead ears of corn are everywhere.

Everyone is dressed up in a costume. There's too much to look at. After all this time, trapped in that apartment with only Dani as my companion, the party and the people are too much for me. My head pounds. I'm far too stimulated by the sights and sounds.

But that's not why I stay on her ass.

I'm guarding it. Too many men—and some women —are paying close attention to it. And it's mine.

I daringly sling an arm around her shoulders, tucking her tight against me as we enter the hall where the party is being held. I already knew how drop dead gorgeous she looks. Once I realize that there were others admiring my woman, I didn't let her get too far from me.

To my delight and surprise, she doesn't seem to mind.

Instead of mingling with her friends and co-workers, she steers me toward the refreshment table. It's a great spot. We can see the band play, but the acoustics are softer in this corner. As we sip on a smoky non-alcoholic punch, Dani and I are able to continue some of the conversations we started back at the apartment.

Turns out we both like to people watch. Rather than be the center of attention, we have a blast standing off to the side, pointing out extravagant costumes and making up backstories for the ones wearing them.

Because Dani is still a recent transplant to Salem, she doesn't know too many people here and that makes our guesses even more fun and ridiculous. As the night goes on, I add her imagination and laugh out loud sense of humor to the list of things I love about her.

A few of her colleagues come over to say hi. None of them stay long. I have Dani all to myself, just the way I like it.

And then—

"Dani! What are you doing, hiding by the punch bowl? I've been looking for you all night! I thought you ditched me."

Two people approach the refreshment table together. The first, a pretty young woman with her fair hair done up in some intricate do. She's wearing a colonial-style dress and her heels are so high, we're almost the same height.

The man accompanying her isn't so lucky. He's probably a head shorter than me. He has on a puffy white shirt and a black cape that hides most of his body. Plastic fangs overhang his thin lips. Beady eyes narrow in immediately on my Dani.

She doesn't seem to notice as she moves away from me, greeting her friend with a hug.

"I would never do that, Allison. I promised I'd come, right?"

Allison. "Oh, so this is Allison?"

"You've heard of me?"

I nod, edging closer to Dani. I don't like her being that far from me, not while this guy is stripping her bare with his gaze. "Dani talks about you all the time. You're her best friend."

"Really? That's weird. She's never mentioned you before."

That's not true. Not exactly. I've overheard countless conversations where Dani told Allison all about me—the *Casper* me.

I open my mouth to correct her when I feel the tip of Dani's heel nudge my ankle. I close my trap.

Allison doesn't notice. With a smile on her pretty face, she's turned her attention on Dani. Her vampire buddy is still staring at Dani, too.

I already hate him.

"Aren't you going to introduce me to..."

Her voice trails off like she doesn't know what to call me.

I stick my hand out. "Hi. I'm Zack, Dani's boyfriend."

"Boyfriend?" Allison echoes as she shakes my hand.

"Friend," Dani corrects. She smacks me in the side with the flat of her hand. I don't mind since, from the sudden glare of the other man's face, I know I got my point across. "Zack's a friend of mine—"

"Close friend," I interject. I don't offer a greeting to the man lurking next to Allison.

"Sure. Anyway, he lives in my building and he didn't have anything to do for Halloween. I didn't think anyone would mind if he tagged along."

Allison's green eyes sparkle mischievously. I know Dani is going to have a lot to answer to her friend for tomorrow. Don't care. For the moment, I'm only worried about tonight.

Tomorrow can wait.

"I didn't know you were bringing a friend."

Dani shrugs. "Last minute decision. Trust me, Allison, neither did I."

The man at Allison's side clears his throat.

She gives a start, as if she forgot he was there. "Oh, right. Dani, this is Ernie. I didn't know about your Zack and, well, I thought..."

I turn my glare on Ernie. Yeah. I know exactly what she thought.

Ernie gives me one quick dismissive look before turning toward Dani. "Allison has told me all about you, Danielle. Maybe when you're done talking to your friend, you can come out on the dance floor with me for a song or two."

He says *friend* like it's a curse. I'm wishing Dani had agreed that I was her boyfriend. I know why she didn't

—what kind of boyfriend can I be when I only can give her one real night—but still.

It's taking all of my self control not to wipe that leer off his face.

What I wouldn't give for a shot of spectral energy right about now. I'd knock this bozo right on his ass and no one could get me for assault.

Since I don't want to spend the rest of my hours with her in a jail cell, I settle on hitting Ernie where it counts.

I wrap my arm around her waist, give her hip a possessive squeeze. "Sorry, Ernie. Dani's dance card is all full up tonight."

He sniffs. "Yes, well, if she changes her mind, I'll be available."

"Make yourself unavailable. She won't change her mind."

Dani bumps into my hold. She doesn't try to break away, though, or say anything to Ernie herself. I know I'm pushing my luck. Just this once, I think she's gonna let me get away with it.

With a puppy dog look in Dani's direction, then a challenging dare in mine, he storms off, swallowed by the gyrating crowd in an instant.

Allison reaches out and takes Dani's hands in hers. "Don't worry about Ernie. I'll smooth things over with him." She glances over at me. "Sorry about that, Zack. If I knew Dani was bringing you, I never would've tried to introduce her to Ernie." Another quick look at Dani. She jerks her head in my direction. "This is something your best friend needs to know about."

Dani's laugh is sweet. "I'll call you first thing in the morning."

"Details, sister. I'm gonna want all of them."

Dani rolls her eyes and shakes her head. "A good girl never kisses and tells."

I feel my back go ramrod straight as other parts of me come to attention. Kissing? Does that mean there's going to be kissing?

Allison giggles and I'm willing to bet it has everything to do with my reaction. Wishing us a good night —adding a sly wink when she says *good*—Allison starts to walk away. Three steps, then she pauses, turns back.

"I'm sorry, Zack. I just have to ask. I know what Dani is supposed to be. Are you... are you wearing a costume?"

Dani stiffens against me. I don't know why. I thought my costume idea was pretty clever. "Yeah. I'm dressed as a mortal."

Dani's friend quirks one of her pencil-thin eyebrows. "Did you just say *mortal*?"

I nod. I gesture at my jeans and faded grey tee. "Just a regular, everyday, not spooky mortal human guy."

"Okay, yeah. I.. I guess I kinda get it."

"YOUR FRIEND DIDN'T GET IT," I TELL DANI AFTER Allison is gone.

"Most people won't." She snorts. It's super cute. "They're used to people dressing up as ghosts for Halloween, not the other way around."

I shrug. "I guess you like his costume better."

"Whose?"

I'm trying to rein in my jealousy. It isn't Dani's fault that that douche was undressing her with his eyes.

Still fuming at the memory, I spit out his name: "*Ernie.*"

"Wait a second. Were you—are you jealous of him? Of *that* guy?"

I don't know why she sounds so incredulous. Why wouldn't I be? He was undressing her with his eyes and tomorrow, when I'm invisible and transparent again, Ernie will still have a chance with my girl.

Dani looks at me like I've lost my mind. "I've never met that guy before in my life. Allison is always trying to set me up with someone and it never works. Remember the one time I brought a guy home?"

How can I forget? I almost lost it entirely when I saw Dani kissing that Ken doll wannabe. It only got worse when I realized that she wasn't into him and he was trying to pressure her into giving something she didn't want to.

If I was alive, I would've killed him. As a ghost, all I could do was scare the shit out of him.

"Yeah," I grumble. "I remember."

She pats me softly in the chest. "That was the moment I realized I shouldn't waste my time with real life guys. They're all jerks. Why bother when I had a good man—a good ghost—waiting for me at home already?" Her smile is coy and a little bit teasing. "Casper might be a perv, but he's *my* perv, and he gave me the best orgasm I ever had."

I immediately look around us, making sure no one overheard her. I'm proud of that night we spent together and I'm stunned to hear her call me hers. Even so, I want to make sure her admission is for me alone.

This moment is ours. And since it might be the only one we'll get, I'm selfish and greedy. I don't want to share.

Come tomorrow, I'll have to. Until next Halloween, at least.

Before I can say anything in response, she trails her hand down my chest, stopping when she reaches the hem of my jeans. I'd give every breath I have left for her to keep on going lower.

Instead, she tilts her head back, looking up at me through the fringe of her lashes.

"Did you mean it?"

"Huh? What?"

I don't know what she's talking about. Doesn't

really matter. The way she's looking up at me? I'm sure I meant every word of it.

Her tinkling laugh goes straight to my throbbing cock. "About the dance card, Zack. Did you mean it?"

Is she actually giving me further permission to touch her, to hold her close, to press our bodies together? I only said it to tick off Ernie, but if Dani is interested?

I'll fucking dance all night.

Dani

The music changes. A jazzy rendition of *I Put A Spell On You* filters in through the room. Zack grabs my hand and pulls me into the middle of the dance floor. Before I can protest and tell him that I was teasing him and that I kind of *don't* dance, he wraps his arms around my waist again and tugs with enough force that our bodies are pressed close together, my back to his front. He takes the lead, swaying to the music as he folds his big body over mine.

He nuzzles my neck with his chin. I shiver. God, that feels amazing.

The hot, hard length of him nestled up against the cleft of my ass as we move?

Even better.

I know how I affect him. Ever since the pillow incident last night, he's made it very clear. I'm willing to bet his cock has been hard ever since he became solid. I still haven't gotten my mind-blowing orgasm out of my head. I suddenly realize that I'm kinda into the idea of returning the favor.

He'll be gone again tomorrow, a simple spirit whose trapped in my apartment. I'm the only link to the living world he has. From the looks some of the guests are giving him, I know he could go home with anyone. The sexy tree in the corner has been giving him "do-me" eyes since we arrived.

I'm surprised at the jealousy bubbling up in the pit of my stomach.

He could probably go home with anyone here.

I want him to go home with me.

You know, I want to blame Allison. Zack, too, I guess. If it wasn't for his caveman act when she brought Ernie over, I don't think it would have really hit me how much he cares. I mean, I should've known from the rose petal, the heart, the little gifts, even his pretty massive—not to mention *constant*—hard-on that he really meant it when he said he loves me.

But to stand there as he staked his claim when we only have one night together?

I've never got so damp, so fast.

We only have one night. I don't want to waste it.

"Zack," I murmur.

"Mmm?"

"We have until midnight, right?"

His grip on my waist tightens. "I think that's how it works."

Halloween. Twenty-four hours. That's all the time we have before he'll have to cross over to the other side again. Maybe he'll come back in a year. I hope he will.

For now, I'll take the time we have.

I trace the lines in his big hand with the tip of my pointer finger. "Remember what happened the other night?"

He goes entirely still. My back is up against his chest. The *thump-thump-thump*ing of his frantically beating heart is the only clue that he heard what I said. Under my ass, I swear I feel the bulge in his jeans twitch.

Oh yeah. He remembers.

I wrap my fingers around two of his and squeeze. "Take me home."

8

A BUMPY RIDE

Zack

I don't give Dani even a second to change her mind. The instant she gives me the go sign, I wrap my arm around her and heft her off the ground. I barely feel her weight at all. My head is pounding, all of my blood rushing to my cock.

And I thought it couldn't get any harder.

Wrong. I was so wrong.

Just the gentle touch of her fingers against my skin had my sac drawing up tight. If I don't get her out of here right away, I might just shame myself by exploding in my jeans.

Dani's laughing as I rush her out to the car. She pulls her car keys out of the tiny handbag she's carrying, clicking the locks off in time for me to open the door and plop her in the driver's seat.

"You sure you want me to drive?" she asks through the crack in her window.

"I was in the car with you on the way here," I remind her as I fling my body into the passenger seat. "Trust me, you'll get us back to your place faster. Right now I'm all about speed."

"Hope you change your mind by the time we get back. Now, strap in, Zack. This might be a bit of a bumpy ride."

She's not kidding, either. Dani drives like a mad woman and I love her even more for it. I can't explain it, don't have any idea how I got so fucking lucky, but she seems as desperate to get back to her place as I am.

Her wheels squeal as she pulls into the parking lot. The car is still running as I spring open the passenger side door, hop out of the car, and run over to her. I wait anxiously for Dani to kill the engine and take out her keys before I open her door, reach inside, and hoist her back in my arms.

I head for the stairs. Elevator might be easier, but this is faster. Dani's giggle carries behind her as I take the stairs two at a time.

We lost her witch's hat somewhere, her long hair cascading down her back. She still has her keys in her hand, though. Before she inserts the key in the lock— and I start having some real dirty thoughts about doing the same with my key and her lock—Dani reaches up with her free hand and lays her palm against my cheek.

I turn to look down at her. I only have a second to think how fucking beautiful she is when she closes the gap between us. Before I know it, her lips are on mine. A second later, I open my mouth and her tongue darts inside. She takes control of the kiss and I love it.

Because this... this is a kiss.

I'm so dazed by the force behind it and the passion in it, I don't realize that she's gotten the door open until Dani nudges me in the side with her foot. I can feel my cheeks flaming up and, though all I want to do is kiss her again, I know better than to do that in the hallway.

Bedroom. Bedroom first.

She kicks the door closed behind her. The slam makes me realize exactly what's going on. And, if I'm *super* lucky, what's about to happen.

The second I set her back on her feet, Dani boldly cups my erection through my jeans. I should probably feel embarrassed at the wet spot that begins to form under her palm, I'm leaking so damn much. Pre-cum soaks through my boxers and into the denim.

Dani does any more exploration, I'm gonna blow my whole load while still wearing pants. With my luck, the stain will carry over when the night ends and my ghostly attire will carry the mark of her touch.

Then again, I really like that idea.

You know what I like even better?

The gleam in her eyes as she drops to one knee, then the next, before reaching out and deftly flicking the button of my jeans open. The roar of the zipper as she tugs it down echoes in my ears.

I'm too stunned to do anything but let her.

Dani reaches into my boxers, freeing my cock in one quick motion.

It takes everything I have not to spill right then and there. The touch of her hand against my bare skin?

Fucking amazing.

She gives me a leisurely stroke before increasing her pace, pumping up and down the length of my shaft.

"You…" I gulp. The words seem stuck in my throat, but I'll hate myself if I don't say them. "You don't have to do that."

There's a devilish twinkle in her eyes. "I don't have to do anything I don't want to."

Then, before I can say or do anything, she dips her head and presses the tip of her tongue to the head of my cock. She gives it a little swirl and, I swear, my eyes roll back in my head. She grabs my cock by the base, circling her tiny fingers around the girth.

The quick tug up and down the length of my shaft has me cursing out loud.

Dani giggles. "See? You're not forcing me to do anything. I *want* to do this."

I get it. I think. My head... it's not working too well at the moment. But I think I get it.

She said something about returning the favor when we were speeding home. It doesn't matter that the moment we shared in her bedroom was more for my pleasure than hers. She thinks she owes me something.

I want to tell her she's wrong. That, if she wants to give me pleasure, she should let me eat out her pussy for real this time.

But then Dani lowers her head again and opens her mouth. Heat envelopes my length, a wet warmth that has my knees quaking and my balls drawing up tight.

Just when I think I can't stand anything else, she starts to suck.

I barely last a minute.

Dani

I don't know who's more surprised when Zack jerks and my mouth fills with his hot cum: him or me. Giving head has never been something I enjoyed, though I'd be lying if I said that his reactions to my touches don't make me feel like the best blower ever or something.

Swallowing his load, I slowly pull back and away from his cock. He's still pretty hard and I'm glad. I've got plans for him. He might've shot his wad a little early, but what did I expect? If it's been a while for me, it's probably been even longer for Zack.

I lick my lips, delighted at his taste. The tang of salt and sweat is replaced by a spicy musk that turns me on even more. I can't help it. Leaning in, I lay the flat of my tongue against his cock and slowly lick again.

Zack shudders, his brawny hands going straight to my shoulders. At first, I think he's repositioning so that he can feed me his dick again. I'm game for it. Then I feel his weight pressing down on me and I realize that he's using me to brace his body.

I sucked all the strength out of him.

"You okay, Zack?"

He pants. I love it. "Just... just give me a sec to recover."

"I hope so," I tell him. Leaning in, I dart my tongue out and give the side of his cock another teasing lick. A bead of pre-cum forms on the tip and I lap that up, too. "That was all about taking the edge off. Then we can start the real fun."

His fingers bite into my skin as he groans again. "God, Dani, you're gonna kill me."

"Then it's a good thing you're already dead," I quip.

Zack stiffens and, for an instant, I think I might've killed the mood with my joke. Did I really need to remind him that this moment isn't going to last forever, no matter how much either of us wants it to?

I want to draw his attention back to me. If his cock is aching to fill something as much as my empty pussy is desperate to be filled, then a tug, a stroke, a tickle should be all it takes to give him something else to focus on.

He starts panting again almost immediately. Muttering filthy curses under his breath, Zack bucks in my hand. I increase the pace, the heat of the friction between our skin only second to the way I'm burning up inside.

With a gasp, almost as if he's surprised to find himself coming again, Zack erupts all over my hand. Hot, sticky cum coats my fingers. Feeling daring, I yank the top of my dress down until more cleavage is showing. With a leisurely swipe, I coat the tops of my tits with his cum.

"Shit, Dani, do you know what you do to me? Seeing you marked that way with my jizz? You're driving me fucking crazy!"

Good. Turnabout's fair play, considering I thought I was nuts for months before I realized my apartment was really haunted.

"You liked that?"

"Baby, I loved it."

"Then wait 'til you see what I have planned for next."

I make quick work of the rest of my dress. The look in Zack's dark eyes tells me that he was seconds away from tearing it off of me and, since this dress belongs to Allison, I have to save it. No way I can explain how it got ripped.

Bad enough I have to admit I lost her hat.

Once I've taken off my bra and panties and I'm standing there completely naked in front of Zack, I give him a few seconds to take it all in before I crook my finger at him and head for my bedroom. It's one thing to give him a quick blowjob in my living room.

For the main event, I want a bed.

He follows me in, like a dog on a leash. Considering he's still softly panting, I'm not too far off base. Zack stares at me like I've got a treat. His eyes are locked on my chest. He licks his lips.

You know what? I guess I do have a treat for him.

Climbing into my bed, I gesture for him to come closer.

As if to leave no doubt in his mind what I want to do in this bed, I ask, "Do you have a condom?"

A second later—when I see the shadow that flits across his handsome face—I want to smack myself. What am I thinking? He's a flippin' ghost, Dani! Even if he managed to materialize with a rubber, it's gotta be expired by now.

Can a ghost knock me up? I doubt it. And it's not like he's carrying any human diseases—he's kind of dead already and I like to think anything he might've had didn't follow him to the other side.

"Forget I asked that. Come on. Drop those pants already and join me in bed."

To my surprise, he stays a couple of feet away from the edge of my bed. Wiping his mouth with the back of his hand, he stares at my naked body hungrily but doesn't make a move to take his clothes off.

"You... you've done enough for me. We don't have to go any farther, do anything else—"

"Are you telling me you don't want to?"

I glance at the opening in his jeans. His weeping cock is pointing straight up at me. He groans, as if in pain. "Not even close."

"Good, because I'm good with going ahead if you are."

Zack moves closer, dropping to his knees before reaching out to grab my hips. I don't know what he's doing at first, but when he positions me so that I'm laying on my back and his face is inches from my clit, I realize he wants to give me oral again.

Normally, I'd be all for that.

Normally, I wouldn't have a deadline.

I glance at the clock on my bedside table. It's already after eleven.

"Not enough time." At least, I hope not. I'm hoping Zack isn't a one-minute wonder. "I'll never forgive myself if I don't get to fuck you at least once. If there's still time before midnight, you can go down on me all you want. Later. Dick now, mouth later."

I think I've finally stunned him this time. You think he would've known better if he's been watching me all this time. I've never once shied away from what I wanted before—and now I want Zack.

When he stays on his knees, watching me like he can't believe what he just heard, I gesture at his body. I'm completely naked while he's still got on all his clothes. That needs to change and now.

"Naked, Zack. I need you stripped in the next couple of seconds otherwise I'll take care of myself without your help."

To prove I mean it, I slip my hand down to my pussy. I barely nudge my folds with a finger when he lunges out, grabbing my hand, stopping me from touching myself.

"No," he growls. "You offered me that cunt and I want it. Two seconds. Give me two seconds, Dani."

"One—*whoa*."

Okay. So maybe I pushed him too far. I forgot how big and strong he is. With one forceful pull, he rips his t-shirt right off, revealing a muscular torso that looks like it's been sculpted from marble.

"Pants," I demand. "Pants now."

He throws the tattered remains of his shirt to the floor. He's more careful with his jeans, either because he doesn't want to damage his incredibly hard cock or because he realizes that, if he ruins his jeans too, he'll be a pantsless ghost until next year.

Either way, he sheds his jeans and his boxers and I have to ball my hands into fists to keep from grabbing his dick when I see the whole thing bobbing over at me.

It's a thing of flippin' beauty. I can't wait to get it inside of me.

Zack has the same idea. Since I'm on my back, he walks on his knees until he's in front of me. With his cock in his hand, he looms over my body until he's all I can see. Our eyes lock. I want to see the look on his face when he enters me the first time.

I gasp when I feel the tip probe at my entrance. I'm so wet, it provides no resistance, but it's been a while and Zack's not a small guy. He takes his time, though, and I'd like to think it's because he's giving me a second to adjust to his size.

Then I see the blissful expression on his face. He's making it last because me giving up my body to him is all he's ever wanted.

I feel another piece of my heart drop into his hand as his cock breaches my pussy.

It's not long before he's seated all the way inside of me. The stretching burns only for a few seconds before the feeling of absolute pleasure pushes any discomfort aside.

I just feel really, really full.

"You doing okay?"

"Less words," I grit out, "more moving."

Zack's chuckle makes my clit throb. I'm just about to tweak it myself, something to take my mind off of his nearness and the fullness down below, when he takes my advice and starts to move.

Whoa. Can he *move*.

He starts out slow, rocking back and forth as he pulls nearly all the way out before shoving his way back in. When I prove that I can take him, matching stroke for stroke, he picks up his pace. I roll my hips, inviting him in. Our skin slaps together.

"Faster," I moan.

He obliges.

There's something about the two of us together. I was amazed by how fast he came after I put my mouth on him. He returns the favor by angling his body in such a way that his cock goes to town on my pussy while his thigh hits right into my clit on every stroke.

My legs are wrapped around his back, my hands clutching his forearms as his frantic pace starts to shift me across the sheets. I feel my orgasm brewing and I use his strength to propel my body faster, basically impaling me on his length.

"Yes, yes, yes." That's just what I need. It's hitting me in the absolute right spot. "Just. Like. That."

It's like a burst of fireworks behind my eyes. I don't even know when I closed them. My whole body screams in release as the orgasm hits like a brick.

As I come down from my climax, I realize that Zack

is still pounding away. His rhythm quickly lifts me back up and I pop from a second, gentler orgasm as he ruts like a beast in heat. He's chasing something—or giving me everything—I don't know, but I hear him chanting my name under his breath as he fucks me.

I cling to his arms and hold on for the ride.

Right when I feel the thread in my lower belly snap for a third time, I feel Zack go rigid. He pauses for only a second, then redoubles his efforts. On a shout, he jerks his body and empties right into me.

He doesn't pull out right away. The two of use stay connected, sweat slicking our skin, this moment in time something no one can take from us. I feel the pulse in Zack's veins, hear the thud in his heart, and I think for a second how terrible it is that it's going to stop any minute now.

His erection goes down some, though he's still hard enough that he keeps his cock buried inside of me. His strength holds out for a few leisurely strokes before his arms give and he collapses on top of me.

Zack's lips find my temple. "Thank you for that."

If I could find my voice, I might've said the same thing to him.

Instead, I struggle to get my own breath back. Zack's weight is comforting, even if it makes it harder for me to get in air.

There's a good chance my ghost boned me to death.

I smile into his chest.

It would be worth it if he did.

MIDNIGHT COMES.

Damn it.

When we realize there's not enough time for another round, Zack gets dressed—well, he climbs back into his jeans, at least. I don't bother. Grabbing an oversized tee and shimmying it on over my head, I follow Zack out of the bedroom and into the living room.

We only have minutes left. Three, if we're lucky.

I don't know what to say. Twenty-four hours ago, he was a ghost, a feeling, a joke with Allison. He was Casper.

And now he's Zack.

How do you say goodbye to a ghost? How do you fall in love with one?

I don't have an answer to that first question.

The second one is easy: you just do.

Crap.

Leave it to me to fall in love with a flippin' ghost.

Zack is staring at the grandfather clock in the corner of my living room. It's an old antique that Allison helped me find when we were first furnishing this apartment. I liked it because it has character.

Now I want to smash it, if only that would stop time.

"One minute left, Dani."

One minute left. I better make it count.

He hasn't taken his eyes off the old clock yet. I shuffle in front of him, tearing his gaze away. Reaching up on my tiptoes, I frame his face with my hands. With the bong of the old grandfather clock ringing in my ear, I kiss him with everything I have.

—*nine*

—*ten*

—*eleven*

I pull back in time to see the tears glistening in his eyes.

"I love you, Dani," he whispers.

"I'll be waiting for you next Halloween," I promise.

Zack's swollen lips quirk up in a small smile.

And then, just as the clock strikes midnight, he's gone.

9

TWO YEARS

Zack

I come to with a gasp.

The first thing I notice is the incessant beeping. It's like a drumbeat in the back of my aching skull.

Taking a deep breath, my nose fills with the stench of industrial cleaner and a really strong disinfectant. Almost *too* clean, like someone is trying to cover up another odor.

My eyes feel like sandbags. It takes all the energy I have to lift my lids. A blinding light sears my retinas. I clamp them shut.

What the hell?

A few minutes go by before I think I have the strength to try again. This time, I crack my eyes open a sliver.

My eyes adjust. And that's when I see that I'm lying down.

I haven't laid down in ages. Ghosts don't sleep.

Confused and disoriented, I glance down my body. There's a pinch in my arm. Is that... is that an IV line inserted in the crook of my elbow? I move to get a better look and notice there's a tug against my chest. With my free hand, I lift up the paper covering my torso and see the countless amount of patches and wires stuck to my skin.

What is going on here?

What's wrong with me?

I don't know.

I don't like it, either.

Grabbing a fistful of the wires, I yank.

And that's when all hell breaks loose.

AT FIRST, THE NURSES AND THE ORDERLIES TRY TO CALM me down. That doesn't work so they threaten to sedate me, and go through with the threat when I try to rip the wires off of my chest again.

Some fancy doctor comes in much later, when I'm groggy and even more confused than before. Whether it's a result of the medicine or not, none of his medical mumbo jumbo makes any sense to me.

Then my family arrives. Mom first, tears streaming

down her face. Dad, whose cheeks are red and ruddy, his eyes suspiciously wet. Emotion overtakes both of them and Dad has to help Mom out when I demand to know what I'm doing strapped down in a hospital bed.

They send my baby brother in to explain everything. Emile is nearly ten years younger than am. The first thing I notice about him? The baby face I remember isn't as young as it once was. Somehow, someway, my baby bro is now a man.

Sitting gingerly at the edge of my bed as if he thinks I'm gonna break, Emile makes me promise that I won't ask questions or interrupt while he tries to make sense of what happened to me. I give him my promise easily because he's the one who has the answers.

And I need those answers.

He tells me quick. I guess he figures it's like a band-aid: do it quick and it won't sting so bad. Smart kid. Doesn't really soften the blow, though.

Two. Years.

I was in a coma for two years.

I was never really dead. I just slept like I was.

The icing on the cake?

I wound up in a coma due to swelling in my brain because, two years ago, I was hit by a bus.

A fucking bus.

They'd given up hope that I'd ever wake up again. Emile tells me that he was certain I'd recover, that my parents refused to pull the plug because they were convinced. I've spent the last two years in a coma, lying flat on my back in a hospital bed while my messed up brain convinced me I was a ghost.

Maybe I was. Talk about an out of body experience.

I remember every detail of what happened to me while I was "dead". From appearing in that apartment to meeting Dani, falling in love with her, then having the best night of my life on Halloween, I remember it all.

I definitely don't remember getting hit by a bus.

Emile is adamant that it happened. Since I'm talking to my brother and I'm hooked up to more wires than I can count, I've got to admit that he's telling the truth.

Still.

Emile pokes me in the knee. When I don't crumble into a million pieces, he scoots closer. "Listen, Zack. The doctors called us a couple of days ago, before you woke up. They didn't want us to get our hopes up, but they said there were signs of brain activity. And..."

I don't like the way he stops talking. "And what?"

"You got hard, dude."

I blink. "What?"

"Seriously. It happened two or three days ago, it's all been a blur. I don't know what these doctors are looking for, but the head guy told Mom and Dad that all this time you've been a limp noodle. Then, all of a sudden, hard."

I have the sudden desire to pull the sheet up over my head. At least Emile is enjoying this. It's clear how much he's missed me, missed having a brother to fuck with.

I don't take that away from him. It... it doesn't seem right to.

With a sigh, I ask, "What else?"

"It happened again."

Of course, it did.

"Mom was here on Halloween. I swear to God, you've never seen a woman so happy to see her adult son get a boner." He gives me a shit-eating grin. "But don't worry, bro. The nurses shuffled her out of here before you creamed your hospital gown."

I don't know if I'm more embarrassed that my body in this bed reacted the same way as I did when I was with Dani in hers or that one of the faceless nurses that keep on coming and going had to clean up my spill and handle my cock.

I promise myself then and there that, when I find Dani again, I won't tell her about that. I'm pretty sure my girl won't be happy to hear another woman had her hands on me, even if I was in a coma.

Because, now that I'm *not* in a coma, Dani is even more my girl. I just have to get the hell out of this hospital bed and find her so that she knows.

Emile is smirking at me. Since I'm still kind of reeling over the fact that Mom saw me get an erection, I throw a hospital pillow at him. He doesn't even bother dodging it. No point. The pillow doesn't even make it halfway to him.

Holy shit, I'm weak.

My dick isn't the only thing that was limp. My arms feel like rubbery noodles. To my utmost embarrassment, they give me a bedpan to use at first since my legs are too weak to stand. I'm so tired, it feels like I could sleep for a year.

Then I remember I did—technically—for two years. And I perk back up.

Emile stays in my room the first two days I'm awake. Mom and Dad keep coming and going. I don't know what they're doing at first and then Dad says that they're talking with my doctors about a game plan going forward.

Considering all I want to do is get up and go see Dani again, I'm not too concerned with all that.

I know I can't tell my family about her. Not yet. They wouldn't understand. Shit, I barely do—and it happened to *me*. The one thing I'm sure of is that my feelings for her didn't die when I came back to life.

If anything, I want her more.

I can't tell my family that I fell in love while I was in a coma. But I do mention that, whatever the game plan they're trying to come up with, all I want to do is go home and get back to living my life.

And that's when Emile admits that my parents had everything moved out of my apartment. When the hospital finally discharges me, I won't be going back to my old place. They all expect me to move back in with my parents.

Hope thuds in my chest at my brother's confession.

My cheesy grin is probably not what Emile is expecting from me. What grown ass man wants to move in with his parents when he's in his early thirties? Even after such a near-fatal accident?

But that's not why I'm smiling. Because, sure, that apartment might not be mine anymore. Doesn't mean that I don't know who it belongs to now.

I'm also positive that that is where I'm going to find Dani.

And that makes my second life that much easier.

THEY KEEP ME IN THE PRIVATE HOSPITAL FOR THE FIRST two weeks of November before moving me to a rehabilitation facility, all on the bus company's dime.

I try to convince my parents that I don't need to go to rehab, but Emile gets tired of our back and forth arguing and shuts me up by taking the compact out of Mom's purse and showing me what I look like.

After two years on a liquid diet, my body has wasted enough that I barely recognize myself in the mirror. And if I can't recognize myself, how can I expect Dani to?

She only saw me as a solid human for one day and I looked the way I did before I ended up in a coma. A big burly guy, muscular frame, tan complexion, five o'clock shadow, and a head of hair most fellas would kill for.

My poor head is almost naked, my hair is buzzed so short. I've lost all color in the two years I've been in the hospital, so I definitely look more like Casper than I do Zack Banks. I've lost a ton of my muscle mass and I can barely walk around my room without getting winded at first.

With what I have in mind when I see Dani again, I know I'll need my strength.

I'm there for five weeks. At first, they try to stick me in a wheelchair but I'm out of that by the third day. Every day I'm growing stronger, getting bigger, and more and more desperate to get out and find my girl.

Five weeks of intense physical therapy, training, and work. I do every damn thing the doctors tell me. My hair starts to grow in, my body fills out, and Emile stops teasing me about my boner after the first time I'm quick enough to slug him in his arm.

IT'S TOWARD THE END OF DECEMBER WHEN MY DOCTORS finally pronounce me fit enough to move back home.

My parents wanted to come pick me up from the rehab center. It's been seven weeks since I woke up. I know the coma scared the shit out of them and they're watching anxiously to see if I'll relapse, but I can't stand the way they keep treating me like a kid.

When Mom said she'd drive me back to her place, I put my foot down. I'd rather walk. She insisted. I flat out denied her. She cried. I relented. Emile shook his head and said he'd drive me over.

I jumped at the chance.

Because I don't have a way to get around on my own. When Emile told me about my accident, he had to admit that my bike was in even worse shape than I was. I at least had a helmet and a hard head so while my injury was bad, my brains didn't end up splattered in the middle of the road.

My bike wasn't so lucky.

I could've called a taxi or something like that. I was on the verge of doing so right before Mom brought out the waterworks and Emile offered up his car to save me from drowning in guilt. I'm glad he did. It suited my plan perfectly.

I don't mind riding with Emile because, the second we drive out of the rehab center's parking lot, I hijack the car.

"Take me home," I tell him.

"What do you think I'm doing?"

I point at the windshield. "Not Mom and Dad's, Emile. See this light? Make a left. I want you to take me home."

"Zack, I don't think—"

Crossing my arms over my chest, I give him a side-eye. Desperate times call for desperate measures. "Remember when you were sixteen and I caught you with the girl next door in Mom and Dad's hot tub? Maybe Mom would like to hear about that, prove I've still got my long term memory."

The look my little brother gives me is a mix between "you wouldn't" and "fuck you", with a dash of an impressed nod thrown in for extra measure. He doesn't say anything, though when he approaches the light, he takes the left.

Emile doesn't need my directions. He takes each turn as we get to it. A giddy buzz is running through my veins, a cocktail of adrenaline and anticipation as I realize that, after all this time, I'm going to see Dani again.

Our conversation is light and easy. We're bullshit-ting back and forth, the way we used to. Emile doesn't bring up the hot tub incident again and neither do I. To be honest, I don't think I would've told Mom anyway.

A jolt of familiarity hits me as Emile pulls up in front of the apartment building. I want to jump out and run for it. Only the *click-click-click* of the hazards and the clearing of Emile's throat keep me from escaping the car.

"Hey, Zack, um, you do remember me telling you that you... uh... you don't live here anymore, don't you?"

No wonder he thinks I'm nuts. That first afternoon, he made sure that I understood that my parents moved me out of the apartment when it became clear that I wouldn't be coming out of the coma any time soon.

Why else would I want to come here if it wasn't my home any longer?

Because I left my fucking heart behind with Dani, that's why.

I clap him on the shoulder. "Don't worry about that. And, look, I'll explain this all to you some other time. Just... just do me this one favor tonight. Okay? If everything goes to plan, you'll understand tomorrow."

He shakes his head. "Mom is gonna have my ass for this. You know that, right?"

I do. "You're the best. I really missed you the most when I was in that coma. For two years."

"You know, playing the coma card is gonna get old, bro."

"But not yet?"

Emile sighs. "Nah. Not yet." And then he smirks, almost as if he has an idea of what's on my mind.

Or maybe he's still remembering his dip in our parent's hot tub.

"I'm gonna be fine," I promise. Opening the car door, I slip out before my brother changes his mind.

"Well, if you're not, I've got bail money stashed away if you need it."

With a laugh, I slap the roof of his car. "Don't wait up for me," I say cheerfully as I start toward the front of the building.

Emile gives me a goodbye salute by honking his horn. I don't even look behind me. My eye is on the prize. I saw Dani's car parked up front when he dropped me off. She's in her apartment.

I have to see her.

I don't want to just walk inside and take the elevator or the stairs to her floor. Not only does that not seem romantic at all, but I don't want to take the chance that she gets one look at me, alive and in the flesh, and starts screaming her head off.

Shielding my eyes against the blinding motley of Christmas lights strung up on individual balconies, I glance around, hoping for some brilliant burst of inspiration. I can feel the winter chill on my hands, my cheeks, my neck. It's fucking cold out here.

I need to find a way inside.

That's when I see the ladder propped up against the building.

Perfect.

10

MISS ME?

Dani

I hate Christmas movies. If it were up to me, the Hallmark channel would change their brand and show horror movies or something in December.

Friday the 13th. Jason. Nightmare on Elm Street.

I don't want to feel happy and hopeful. As the days pass, I want my ghost back.

I'm not being fair. I know that. Every other holiday season, I'm the first one to binge-watch all those cheesy feel-good romance movies. I used to live for the 25 days of Christmas. Half the time the love stories were unbelievable and full of every trope—friends to lovers, enemies to lovers, fake fiancé, you name it—but I couldn't help but watch and cheer and hope that, maybe one day, I'd have my own unrealistic love story.

Falling in love with a ghost on Halloween is as unrealistic as it can get.

Still happened, though. I fell in love with Zack somewhere between the time I found out he was Casper and the time I had to say goodbye. After that, watching Christmas flicks just made me bitter and moody.

I got my Halloween magic. Is it a little too much to wish for some Christmas magic, too?

To make it worse, some part of me expected Zack to linger even after he faded away. He said he was tied to my apartment—though his choice to "haunt" it was his way of letting me know that he was there—and I kind of thought I'd still sense him, like I did with Casper before.

Nope.

No more rose petals. No hearts drawn in a messy spill. If I lose my keys, they're gone.

Just like Zack.

Ugh.

On my television, sleigh bells jingle. Some version of Santa Claus makes his requisite visit. There's laughter. The indescribably beautiful blonde female lead leans in to accept a kiss from the boringly handsome male lead.

They might've only known each other a week, but they're both sure this is true love. On the Hallmark channel, everyone gets their happily ever after.

Why can't I? I only got to know Zack for one night and I'm already convinced he's the one for me.

Standing up abruptly, I shake my head. God, I'm pathetic.

I'm torturing myself. I know it. Trying to prove that I can move on without him here. It's already been almost two months since that one night changed my life.

There's nothing I can do but wait until next October.

Which means getting through Christmas first. Then New Years. Valentine's Day. I cringe. After that, there's still *eight more months* until Halloween.

I'm never gonna make it.

I slap my hand on the power button. The cable box blinks off, the television going black with a soft *pop*.

And that's when I hear it.

Rap, tap, tap.

Knocking.

I hold my breath.

That... that's not coming from the front door.

My heart stops beating for a second.

Rap, tap, tap.

I'm stunned, bare feet frozen to my floor. Hope fills me up like a balloon. The gentle tapping sounds like it's against glass. The direction is definitely coming from the other side of the room.

There's no way—

It's not possible—

I almost don't check. In the last few weeks, I've driven myself a little batty, running out to check the balcony every couple of nights as if I'll miraculously find Zack standing there. It's usually the winter wind, or a bird tapping at the glass. It's never him.

Then again, that really did sound like knocking.

Trying not to get my hopes up too high, I tiptoe toward the balcony. The week after Halloween, I went out and bought a curtain rod plus a set of floor-length curtains. I needed to block that part of the apartment off. If I couldn't see the balcony, it might help me stop obsessing over my missing ghost lover.

It's with a shaky hand that I grab one of the curtain panels and tug.

And there he is.

"Zack?"

Since that magical Halloween night, I've imagined a scene like this a million times. As much as I hated them, watching Christmas flick after Christmas flick built up a prayer in me that I was hoping would be answered.

Now that is has been, I stand there like a dope, staring.

He's here.

And he's flippin' gorgeous.

His hair is shorter than it was, his skin a little more pale, and there's dark circles under his eyes that probably match mine. The minor imperfections, though, make him all the more stunning. Because he's here and he's real and not the least bit see-through.

A hesitant smile tugs at his lips. His dark eyes are gleaming as he gazes down at me. The Christmas lights I haphazardly strung along the railing of the balcony glimmer and shine behind him, throwing a soft golden halo around his body.

My breath catches in my throat. In an instant, I wonder if I'm seeing him now because he's an angel, not a man.

Is this... is this goodbye again?

Before I can burst into tears—my overactive imagination has already convinced me that this is Zack telling me he's off to Heaven or something—he offers me a small shrug and a sheepish grin.

"Hi, Dani. Um... it's kinda chilly out here and I sort of forgot my coat in my rush to see you at last. Do you —can I come in maybe?"

Holy hell. What is *wrong* with me?

I rush forward, fingers fumbling with the lock, cursing wildly under my breath as I struggle to get the darn door open.

He's chuckling as I slide the glass door back, his eyes bright and shining and alive. The moment there's a few inches gap in the doorway, Zack slips his hand inside and shoves the glass before rushing into the apartment. Cool skin—because it's December, not because he's dead—shocks my bare arms as he grabs me, pulling me close.

I wrap my arms around his torso and tilt my head back, offering my lips to him invitingly. He's not a ghost, so maybe he is an angel, but either way he can touch me and I damn well want to make sure that I'm touching him back while I can.

Zack doesn't hesitate. Swooping down, his chilly lips find mine. Within seconds, we're both on fire. I kiss him with everything I have, as if we break apart again, he'll vanish like he did on Halloween.

My hands are like velcro, they're stuck tight behind his back. No one could pry me away from him if they tried. He's back and I'm not about to let him go.

This doesn't make any sense to me, though I have to say that sense flew out the window the second I accepted that my apartment was haunted. I don't want to ask questions—I'm afraid if I do, I might wake up and find this is a dream—but staying quiet isn't who I am.

I have to know. So, in between kisses, I shoot frantic questions at him.

"How is this possible?" I demand. "Are you really here? What's going on? Are you an angel? Are you alive? How did this happen?"

Zack's chuckle, the deep rumble of it, hits me right in the heart, before traveling due south. God, I love that sound.

"Miss me?"

He has no idea how much.

I clear my throat, trying to compose myself. It's hard. These last few weeks have been very, very rough.

Tears well up anyway. "The day after Halloween, I thought I would still sense you. Maybe there'd be a sign—another flower petal, a message in my mirror, something. But you were gone and... and now you're here. I just... *how*?"

And he tells me how he wasn't really a ghost because he hadn't actually died and it was really a coma so he's definitely not an angel and I kind of don't hear what he says after that because he's here and he's alive and I can feel the heat of his erection against my thigh and I wanted him *yesterday.*

Christmas has come early for me and I'm not about to waste this gift.

Yay Christmas magic!

"You know what? Forget all that. You're here now—"

He kisses me again. "And I'm not going anywhere without you again."

Sounds good to me. I latch onto the sexy scruff on his jaw, kissing him so deeply that we're sharing the same breath. Without realizing it, I started rotating my hips, grinding on his erection, using his hard length and the friction of his jeans to give my clit a little action.

I need more of this. I need more of him.

My Zack.

Shimmying down his body, I land on the floor with a soft *thump* and immediately start to back up towards my bedroom. "Let's go."

It takes him a second to realize that I'm not in his arms any longer. His lips are red and a little swollen from the passion and the force of my kisses.

I think I've kissed him stupid, since he looks at me with a dazed expression.

"Huh? Go where?"

"Where do you think? You're here. You're hard. You fucked the brains out of my head on Halloween and I thought I had to wait a year for you to do it again. I don't want to waste any time in case you vanish." I gesture at him, wagging my finger at his jeans. "Come on. Take your pants off."

"Dani, sweetheart, I'm not going anywhere. Didn't you hear me? I'm... I'm alive."

"I see. I'm really glad, too, but didn't you hear me? Pants. Off. Now."

He doesn't move.

Does he need a little push? I remember the night we first got together and how hesitant he was until I basically dropped to my knees and freed his cock myself. It was like he didn't believe that I'd be into him until I showed him how wrong he was.

Reaching down, I grab my shirt by the hem and rip

it over my head and off. He doesn't want to strip on his own? I'll go first.

His eyes zero in on my chest. Licking his lips, he reaches out with one of his hands and gives my boob a gentle squeeze. A tingle goes through me and, shivering, I reach behind me and unhook my bra. It falls to the floor, leaving me bare under his suddenly heated gaze.

I give my shoulders a shake, making my tits bounce.

How can he say no to this?

"Fuck me," I demand.

Zack lips his licks again, then shakes his head.

"I won't fuck you, Dani."

What? Why?

It's all he wanted to do the last time we were together, and all I've been dying to do ever since he left me. I was thinking I had to wait until next Halloween to have a night with my ghostly lover. Now that he's here and I'm half-naked and panting, he tells me he won't fuck me. Seriously?

Before I can start worrying that he doesn't want me now that he's, well, alive, Zack reaches out and pulls me into his embrace. The warmth of his arms, the steady beat of his heart, that smell that is just so uniquely him... it's Zack. He's here.

He's real.

And from the hot, hard cock pressing up against

the vee of my legs, I know he really wants me as much as I really, really want him.

My stiff nipples chafe against the softness of his shirt. I moan and feel him shudder in response to the sound.

Leaning in, he presses his lips against my ear. His whiskers brush against the sensitive skin, the mild burn going straight to my pussy.

His voice is that sexy rasp I remember from our first night together. Casper—Zack—my fantasy man brought back to life just for me.

"I won't fuck you, Dani," he whispers, "but I will make love to you. Tonight, tomorrow, and for the rest of our lives."

My heart soars. "What about Halloween?"

He reaches down, strong fingers unclasping the button on my jeans. A seductive purr fills his voice as he slowly lowers the zipper. "Especially on Halloween," he promises.

And, to my absolute delight, he does just that.

AUTHOR'S NOTE

Thank you for reading *Halloween Boo*!

I've always been a huge fan of Halloween. I first saw *Hocus Pocus* when I was 10 and it was initially out in the theater... twenty-five years ago *cringe*. I might not have understand all of the jokes and innuendos then, but as it is my annual go-to film to get in the spirit of Halloween, I've seen it hundreds of times (if not more). Recently, I introduced it my 2 1/2 year old niece and nephew. Figuring there's still a few more years before I have to explain to their mother what I have them watching—for now, they love Binx and Billy—I was inspired with an idea that quickly blossomed into this short.

So, in case it wasn't obvious, the *Hocus Pocus* references, among a ton of other pop culture ones, were all intentional. And I hope you enjoyed this as much as I did writing it!

Last Christmas, I gave you my heart. The very next day you... stomped it into a million pieces and left town without a backward glance.

Jerk.

Allison

I know that's not how the song goes. But, for me, that's exactly what happened. I met the man of my dreams on Christmas Eve. We shared one magical night of passion and I thought—well, it doesn't matter what I thought. Because, Christmas morning, he left me under the mistletoe and I never heard from him again.

Until he shows up at my best friend's apartment in the middle of December this year. And I discover that not only did I not know my mystery lover's true name, I never knew his identity, either.

The one night stand I had last Christmas? He's one of the partners for the firm I work for. So he's my boss.

Even worse?

He's my best friend's brother.

Max

It's tough running a company. There's no time for anything—and that includes falling in love. I haven't been in a relationship in over a decade. It never used to bother me, though.

And then I met her.

With long legs, bright green eyes, and a body built for sin, I abandoned my "no distractions" policy and had my wicked way with her for the night. It didn't take long for me to realize that I wanted more than that—but an emergency call had me on the first flight out of Salem.

By the time I could return to search out my Christmas lover, I realized that the number she gave me was fake. The name I moaned? It's not hers.

I don't know why that bothers me so much considering I lied about my own.

Now she wants nothing to do with me. I don't blame her.

Doesn't mean that I'm going back to California without a fight.

———

This Christmas is the second book in the *Holiday Hunk* series and a companion to *Halloween Boo*.

Available now!

After my mate rejected me, I wanted to kill him. Instead, I ran away—which nearly killed *me*...

A year ago, everything was different. I had just left my home, joining the infamous Mountainside Pack. The daughter of an omega wolf, I've always been prized -- but just not as prized as I would be if my new packmates found out my secret.

But then my fated mate—Mountainside's Alpha—rejects me in front of his whole pack council and my secret gets out, I realize I only have one option. Going lone wolf is the only choice I've got, and I take it.

Now I live in Muncie, hiding in plain sight. If the wolves ever left the mountains surrounding the city, I'd be in big trouble. Luckily, the truce between the vampires and my people is shaky at best and Muncie? It's total vamp territory. Thanks to my new vamp roomie, I get a pass, and I try to forget all about the call of the wolf. It's tough, though. I... I just can't forget my embarrassment—and my anger—from that night.

And then *he* shows up and my chance at forgetting flies out the damn wind.

Ryker Wolfson. He was supposed to be my fated mate, but he chose his pack over our bond. At least, he did—but now that he knows what I've been hiding, he wants me back.

But doesn't he remember?

I told him I'll never be his mate, and there isn't a single thing he can do to change my mind.

To Ryker, that sounds like a challenge. And if there's one thing I know about wolf shifters, it's that they can never resist a challenge.

Just like I'm finding it more difficult than I should to resist *him*.

---

* *Never His Mate* is the first novel in the *Claw and Fang* series. It's a steamy rejected mates shifter romance, and though the hero eventually realizes his mistake, the fierce, independent heroine isn't the sweet wolf everyone thinks she's supposed to be...

Get it now!

KEEP IN TOUCH

Stay tuned for what's coming up next! Sign up for my mailing list for news, promotions, upcoming releases, and more!

Sarah Spade's Stories

And make sure to check out my Facebook page for all release news:

http://facebook.com/sarahspadebooks

Sarah Spade is a pen name that I used specifically to write these holiday-based novellas (as well as a few books that will be coming out in the future). If you're interested in reading other books that I've written (romantic suspense, Greek mythology-based romance, shifters/vampires/witches romance, and fae romance), check out my other author account here:

http://amazon.com/author/jessicalynch

Of Mistletoe and Mating

No Way

Season of the Witch

Rogue

Sunglasses at Night

Ain't No Angel *free*

True Angel

Ghost of Jealousy

Night Angel

Broken Wings

Lost Angel

Born to Run

Ordinance 7304: Books 1-3

Printed in Great Britain
by Amazon